It's all Greek at Sea!

Debbie Ward

Copyright © 2017 Debbie Ward

All rights reserved, including the right to reproduce this book, or portions thereof in any form. No part of this text may be reproduced, transmitted, downloaded, decompiled, reverse engineered, or stored, in any form or introduced into any information storage and retrieval system, in any form or by any means, whether electronic or mechanical without the express written permission of the author.

This is a work of fiction. Names and characters are the product of the author's imagination and any resemblance to actual persons, living or dead, is entirely coincidental.

The views expressed in this work are solely those of the author and do not necessarily reflect the views of the publisher, and the publisher hereby disclaims any responsibility for them.

ISBN: 978-1-365-83191-1

PublishNation, London
www.publishnation.co.uk

Thank you to my wonderful husband, Dave who's had to put up with my constant ramblings about characters and plots.

To my very good friend Sally (and no, I did not base my main character on her!) – thank-you for being my sounding board and giving me the confidence to finish this book.

For my amazing Mum, without who I wouldn't be here to write this – I hope that they have books in heaven so you can read this!

Chapter 1

Sally had never been on a cruise before. She had been on a cross channel ferry from Dover to Calais on the famous "booze cruise", and she had sailed around the shores of Corfu on a "sunset cruise" but she had never been on a vessel the size of the monster that stood in front of her now. In fact she had never even seen a ship the size of the one she was now waiting to board and was starting to worry that maybe a cruise round the Med may not have been such a good idea after all!

The idea of a cruise had grown after Sally had started watching a documentary on TV about the crew on one of the big ships and had fell in love with the idea of sailing around the Med. Her husband, Mike, promised her faithfully that he would take her on a cruise one day and that day came sooner than expected when Mike unexpectedly got made redundant from his job as a Warehouse Manager at a large DIY company.

They decided that they would splash out on a "holiday of a lifetime" with some of his redundancy money, so long as he got another job within a reasonable time. With a bit of luck it would also coincide with Sally's 50th birthday in September, which pleased her no end as it would give her the perfect excuse not to have to throw a party and admit to everyone she was getting old!

Mike had been working for the same company for over 30 years and so got a pretty decent pay off. Although there wasn't any real urgency to find another job, he didn't want to fritter the money away on day to day living, so he started applying for jobs pretty much straight away. But unfortunately, just as he had started getting interviews, everything had to be put on hold after his Dad had a heart attack and he went to stay with him in Norfolk for a while to help him recuperate.

Originally from Essex, Mike's Mum and Dad relocated to Norfolk when Mike was about 12. His Dad, Derek, was offered a job running a machinery plant just outside Norwich and they decided it was too good an offer to turn down. They sold their pokey 2 bed flat in Romford and bought a 3 bedroomed bungalow with beautiful gardens, in a sleepy village not far from the Coast. Both Mike and his Mum, Pat, never really took to the country way of life and Mike moved back down to Essex soon after he had finished college.

Not long after, Derek and Pat split up and Pat also moved back down to Essex. Derek, however, loved the country and fitted in as if he'd lived there all his life. He eventually married again, to Sue, who worked in the offices of his firm. Sue had a daughter, Mia, who was at university in Lincoln. Tragically both Mia and her Mum died in a car accident one night when Sue was taking her back to university after staying with them for the summer holidays. Derek never really got over this and has lived alone ever since, with just his dog for company.

Mike got the call that his Dad had been rushed to hospital after suffering a heart attack, one snowy afternoon in late February and he and Sally drove to the hospital in Norfolk straight away, both of them fearing the worst. Luckily it wasn't a massive heart attack but they kept him in hospital for a couple of days and then advised complete rest for the next few weeks. As Derek lived on his own, Mike decided that it would be best if he stayed in Norfolk to be with him for a few weeks, while Sally came back home for work. After all, it wasn't as if he had to rush back for work or anything and he could still keep applying for jobs while he was taking care of his Dad.

After a couple of weeks at home on her own, Sally decided that, after having had a hectic few months at work she could really do with recharging her batteries and so arranged for a month off without pay to go to Norfolk and keep Mike company. Luckily her boss at the legal firm where she worked, was very understanding and let her have the time off straight away. Derek was home from hospital by then and well on the mend so they mainly spent their days going to the coast and taking Bruno, his faithful cocker spaniel, for long walks along the beach and if the weather wasn't too good they spent their time sitting indoors, watching old movies. By the time Sally's month was up, she felt totally relaxed and re-energised. Little did she know what was just around the corner for her!

They both returned home on the Saturday of the first bank holiday weekend in May, ready for Sally to start back at work on the Tuesday. Whilst in Norfolk, Mike had been offered a job at a rival DIY firm in Romford and was due to start there as a Senior Warehouse Manager the following week. They were just giving the house a bit of a clean after being away for so long when Sally got a call from her Aunt Jeannie to say that Sally's Mum, June, had collapsed while they were out shopping and was on her way to the hospital. By the time Sally and Mike had got to the Hospital, which was only 15 minutes away, June was in a coma after suffering a massive stroke. They sat with her all night but she never regained consciousness and died early the next morning.

Sally was devastated. Her Mum hadn't even been ill. It was such a shock and she got through the next few days in a complete fog. Mike and his mum, Pat helped her organise the funeral, which thankfully went without a hitch, then Sally completely withdrew into herself. For several weeks she just sat around staring into space, losing hours at a time, hardly sleeping or eating. She wouldn't see a doctor, apart from getting signed off from work, and wouldn't speak to anyone about it, even her good friend Karen, who came round nearly every evening after work to try and cheer her up. Mike was so worried about her but he didn't know what to do.

Her grief finally broke one evening when she and Mike were going through some family photos and videos. A video of a party where June had got slightly tipsy and ended up doing a really bad Karaoke version of Celine Dion's, My Heart Will Go On, finally had Sally laughing. This turned to tears and she eventually cried herself out and slept right round the clock. The next morning she felt as if a mist had lifted and, although she still missed her Mum like crazy, she knew she had to get on with her life.

In her will, June had left everything to Sally, being her only child. Even though Sally would have given it all to have her Mum back, she still had to face facts that she was now quite well off. The family home was worth around £260,000 and there was some shares that June bought when she was working at the bank. They were now worth around £25,000, not to mention her jewellery and other bits and bobs.

Luckily the house sold pretty much as soon as it went on the market, which was one advantage of living in Essex and being so close to the City. As it was sold to a cash buyer and there was no chain, the whole process took just over 4 weeks. Once everything was finalised, and she had paid off the mortgage on her and Mike's house, Sally had around £200,000 in her bank account and a mortgage free house.

When her boss called her and asked when she was thinking of coming back to work, she decided that she would hand her notice in then and there. Her job, as a legal secretary, was quite stressful and, as she didn't actually need the money at the moment, she decided to take time out and get her head together. If, at some point in the future, she wanted to go back to work, she could always get herself a part time job nearer home.

Mike was delighted that she would be at home for the foreseeable future and he suggested that perhaps now was time that they booked that cruise. A bit of sun, sea, good food and wine would do them both the power of good after the last few months that they had just been through. Although if she didn't think she was up to it, Mike was quite happy to just book a week in Cyprus to go and stay with his daughter Lucy, who lived just outside Paphos and had done for a couple of years now, since marrying Pavlos, a Greek Cypriot that she had met on holiday. They both tried to get out there when they could and, now that Sally had given up work, hopefully they could go out more often. Sally agreed that she did need a holiday so they headed off straight away to book something.

When they got to the travel agents, they both headed to the counter to chat to the agent whose badge indicated that he was a "cruise specialist", even though he only actually looked about 16! The baby-faced, travel agent, whose name was Dean, promised to find them the perfect cruise, however, the only one they had available at this short notice was the Greek Island Cruise on the Grecian Princess which sailed out of Corfu on 30th August. Sally and Mike both thought this was perfect and would also coincide with Sally's birthday which was on 10th September. There were only a few decent cabins available so they booked it there and then. With only 2 weeks until they flew out to Greece they started frantically preparing for their holiday.

Preparations were made a lot easier with Sally not being at work but, by the time she had bought a couple of ball gowns, ordered Mike's dinner suit for their formal nights then bought loads more clothes to go away with, ordered some euros, bought all their toiletries and then packed it all, she was frazzled and was definitely in need of a holiday!

Luckily she managed to get booked in for a haircut as she had completely neglected herself the last few months. Her hairdresser cut her chestnut brown hair into a flattering bob that fell in layers, framing her face and making her look years younger than her impending 50th. He completed her look with some delicate blonde highlights that would really stand out once she got in the sun. She left the hairdressers and went straight into her local beauticians where she had her nails done and got waxed within inches of her life. Feeling completely transformed, she had a renewed bounce in her step as she returned home to finish her last minute packing.

Chapter 2

The day of their much needed holiday came round soon enough and, before they knew it they were descending the steps of the plane at Corfu Airport into the blazing hot sunshine. As there had been a pretty much non-existent summer at home, the heat really hit them.

'Blimey, how hot is that' said Sally, frantically fanning herself with her passport as they walked across to the bus that was waiting to ferry them to the terminal. 'I'm so glad I bought a load of high factor sun cream, I think we're going to need it'

'Don't you dare moan about how hot it is' laughed Mike as he tried strap hanging whilst holding on to his passport, pull along case and carrier bag of "essentials" that Sally had insisted they buy at the airport! 'You really would think, in this day and age, that there would be a better way of travelling wouldn't you, rather than herding you in like a load of flaming cattle'

'Sorry, who's moaning now? And no, I'm definitely not complaining about the heat. This is wonderful after the crap weather we've had this year. I just can't wait to get on that ship, dump all this lot and get myself a nice cold drink'

'I'm sure it won't be long now, Sal. Just got to get through Passport Control and then get on the coach to the cruise terminal. It's weird knowing that our cases are already on the way to the ship. I think I might actually miss standing around in the terminal waiting forever for our cases to come off – not! This is a much more civilised way of doing things'

It was actually quite a breeze getting through the airport and in less than half an hour they were sat on the coach and on their way to the cruise terminal. The journey only took 15 minutes and it gave Mike and Sally a chance to cool down in the air conditioning whilst gazing out to the turquoise sea, sparkling in the midday sun.

As they pulled into the cruise terminal, Sally could see the "Grecian Princess" in all her splendour.

'Flipping hell, I didn't think it would be that big, did you?' asked Sally, starting to worry about how something that size would stay afloat.

'Well I did have an idea that we weren't going on a cross channel ferry' teased Mike. 'I'm sure it won't seem quite so big once we're on it'

'Mm, maybe' said Sally, not quite convinced.

They pulled up at the terminal entrance and walked inside. As their cases had already been transferred onto the ship, all they had to do was wait for their allocated number to be called so they could start the boarding process. Mike decided that he needed to use the loo so Sally stood with their hand luggage by a large window overlooking the ship. She was definitely starting to get worried about this cruise and really wished that they had booked to visit Lucy in Cyprus instead.

'Oh for God's sake woman, pull yourself together' she scolded herself, a little too loudly. 'It's only a bloody ship, what's the worst that could happen?'

'I'm sure the passengers waiting to board the Titanic had exactly the same thoughts as you my dear' piped up an elderly lady who was standing next to Sally, complete with one of those push a long trolley things that seems to be the fashion accessory of choice nowadays for the over 70's!

'Not really the reassurance I was looking for to be honest' muttered Sally, desperately looking round for her errant husband, who always managed to slope off to the loo at the most inopportune times.

'Obviously a cruise virgin then!' piped up trolley lady again! 'You'll be fine once you've done your first one. Then you'll be like me and George here. What is it now George, our 20th or 30th cruise?' she carried on without waiting for George to answer! 'I forget, we've done so many, haven't we dear? Well, if there's anything you need to know about the ship or any of the ports, then I'm sure one of us will be able to put you right. I think we actually know more than the staff, who incidentally seem to be getting younger and younger these days! Oh by the way, I'm Prudence and this is my husband George, we're staying in one of the suites on the Spa Deck. You're not on your own dear are you?'

'Pleased to meet you, I'm Sally and, no I'm not on my own, my husband Mike has decided to go walkabout but I'm sure he'll be back any minute.' said Sally, who was now really wishing that they'd booked anywhere but here, and not decided to splash out on a "once in a lifetime" holiday like this.

Luckily, just as Prudence was just about to launch into another tirade, Sally's missing husband Mike made his way back from the Gents.

'Hi sweetheart, see you've made friends already then' said Mike jokingly as he saw Sally making faces behind trolley lady and her lapdog husband!

'Very funny Mike. Where the hell have you been? I thought you said you were going for a pee, you've been gone more than half an hour. Even you can't pee for that long'

'Well' grinned Mike sheepishly. 'I did start chatting to a bloke in the loo, as you do, and it's his first cruise as well. Anyway, he looked a bit worried about it all so I said that we'd meet him and his wife in the bar this evening for a drink. Hope you don't mind!'

'Doesn't really matter if I do, does it, seeing as you've already made arrangements. I wouldn't have minded having a bit of a mooch around the ship tonight and just going where the mood took us but, hey ho! Actually, no, I don't mean that, of course it's all right, I'm just getting a bit nervous about getting on board. Talking of which, our number is on the screen, it looks like we might be boarding soon'

'Think you'll find it's embarking, babe, not boarding. We're going on a ship not a plane'

'Whatever! Let's just get on the flaming thing, get unpacked and find the nearest bar. I can feel a large G & T calling to me!'

Chapter 3

The embarkation process, much to Sally and Mike's amazement, was really straightforward and within minutes they were walking into the central atrium of the "Grecian Princess" where all Sally's previous worries about the ship disappeared.

'Wow' exclaimed Sally and Mike at the same time, both standing with their mouths open in amazement.

'Blimey, I knew it was going to be special' said Mike craning his neck to take in the vast size of the atrium 'but this is something else. It'll take us a week to find our way round the place. It's enormous!'

Sally and Mike spent the next hour wandering around, oohing and arhhing at everything they saw, until the Captain announced over the tannoy that the cabins were now ready to go to.

Their cabin was on C Deck, half way down the ship and right in the middle, which according to most people on the cruise forums, was most probably one of the best places you can be on a ship, especially for stability, which is why Mike picked it, as he didn't have the best sea legs in the world! They managed to find it easily enough and their pile of bright pink suitcases, another one of Sally's must have purchases, were waiting for them outside the door.

They were both really impressed with the cabin. It was much bigger than they expected with a queen sized bed as well as a sofa and a large coffee table, which would come in handy for when they had room service some mornings instead of going down for breakfast. There was tea and coffee making equipment and a selection of biscuits, which Mike wasted no time in tucking into, whilst Sally soon commandeered the dressing table for her many lotions, potions and bags of make-up and hair paraphernalia. There was also a flat screen television on the wall opposite the deceptively comfortable sofa and a small fridge for their wine.

The bathroom was small but compact, with a shower cubicle, toilet and vanity unit with plenty of shelving to put toiletries. It wasn't the largest bathroom they had stayed in but it looked like it would do the job.

The one thing they both got excited about was the amount of hanging space available. There was a large rail outside the bathroom with room under it to put several pairs of shoes and a shelf above to put their bags. It also had the addition of a floor to ceiling cupboard containing a digital safe and even more shelving. With the amount of luggage they had bought with them, this was the answer to their prayers!

Before unpacking their umpteen cases, holdalls and bags, they both went out on the balcony to have a look and get some air. This again was a lot bigger than they expected and was furnished with a couple of reclining sun loungers and a small table. It afforded them an amazing view of the port at Corfu and they were glad that they paid that little bit extra for it and not just settled on an outside cabin, which Dean in the travel agency originally suggested.

'I think this cruising lark was a good idea of mine, don't you?' asked Mike as he plonked himself in one of the loungers and put his feet up. 'I have a feeling I could get used to this'.

'Well before you do, I think you'd better give me a hand to unpack some of this lot' said Sally pointing to the mass of luggage waiting for them inside. 'Oh OK' groaned Mike dragging himself off the sun lounger. 'I suppose I'd better do as I'm told or I'll never hear the last of it'

'Funny, I don't think' replied Sally lobbing an unopened packet of holiday pants at him!

After about an hour of unpacking and putting everything in its rightful place, the cabin was starting to look quite homely. It was amazing how much room there was, especially considering the amount of clothes they had brought with them! Luckily Sally had the forethought to pre-book extra luggage with the airline before they went away otherwise the excess baggage charges at Gatwick would have been extortionate.

Just as they were about to go off and explore there was a knock on the door. Mike opened it to a jolly Indian man who informed them that his name was Wilson and that he was their cabin steward. He wanted to make their acquaintance and to let them know that if there was anything they needed, day or night, just to call him and he would deliver it personally. Mike and Sally introduced themselves and told him that they were very pleased to meet him but not to expect too many calls from them as they were sure that they had everything they needed.

'That was really sweet of him to introduce himself to us wasn't it' said Sally as they finally got out of the cabin and started walking down the corridor towards the lift.

'Yeah it was' agreed Mike. 'But I'm sure he's gone round all his allotted cabins doing exactly the same thing. The friendlier he is, the more tips he'll get!'

'God, you're such a cynic Mike, you always assume everyone's got an ulterior motive. Why can't they just be friendly?'

'Oh I'm sure he is friendly but you have to be a bit realistic Sal, he's not doing this job for fun, he's doing it to send money back home to his family. So it makes sense that the more he gets people to like him, the more money they are likely to give him at the end of the cruise and ... Oh my God, look at that!'

Sally looked up to what Mike was now staring at open mouthed, and laughed.

'Trust you to find the menu. What's on tonight, anything worth having?'

'Anything worth having. I'd have the bloody lot given half a chance' said Mike, almost salivating over the menu that was on the wall outside the main dining room. 'I can see us having to jog round the ship after eating all this, otherwise we'll be waddling off!'

'Ooh look Mike, they've got duck on there. I love that. Oh and risotto for starter and just look at the desserts. Yeah I think you're right about jogging round the ship, though perhaps a brisk walk may just have to do!'

'Well at least we won't starve on here. I can't believe the amount of choice there is'

Mike was right, there were several eateries dotted around the ship. In addition to Delphi and Olympia, the two buffet restaurants that were situated one at each end of the ship, and the two main dining rooms, The Parthenon and The Acropolis which both served off the same menu, there was also The Dionyssis Grill House. All five of these restaurants were in with the price paid for the cruise but, if you fancied something a little bit special, then there was Pandesia

Greek Taverna, The Blue Room and Crystal, all of which had a supplement attached to them, ranging from £5 to £50 extra, per person. And if none of those appealed to you, there was always 24 hour room service!

After spending the best part of an hour looking at menus outside the different restaurants, they headed back to their cabin to collect their life jackets in readiness for Muster which was to be held in the Aphrodite Bar at 4.30 sharp. By 5pm they knew exactly what to do in an emergency, where the life boats were and how to put on a life jacket, which hopefully they'd never have to put to the test.

On their way back to the cabin to start getting ready for the evening, they had a quick stop off at the coffee shop where they both demolished a hot chocolate with whipped cream and marshmallows, plus a large slice of carrot cake – just to keep them going until dinner time!

'Quick get down' hissed Sally as Mike was just about to stand up. 'It's that bloody Prudence woman again. I don't want to get lumbered with her and her lap dog husband again. I had enough of her before we got on here. They're certainly not the sort of people I want to be associating with on here. Talk about up their own bloody arses!'

'It's OK she's gone past' said Mike getting up. 'That'll teach you to start talking to weirdos when I'm not about! Actually, she really reminds me of that Mrs Bucket woman on the telly. You know, the bossy, snobby one, what's her name?'

'Oh, you mean Hyacinth Bouquet. Blimey, you're right she does, doesn't she.'

'Yeah, she really does' laughed Mike. 'Anyway, enough of all this frivolity, we'd better get back and start getting ready. Don't forget we're meeting that couple I told you about'

'Oh no' Sally rolled her eyes towards heaven as she remembered the meeting that Mike had kindly arranged for them. 'I'd forgotten about that. Right then, while you're having a shower I'm going to Facebook Karen to see how she is. That bloody bloke she's been seeing has taken himself off on a lads' only golfing holiday – or so he says! I really don't trust him myself but what can you do. She obviously thinks he's the "bees' knees". I've never actually met him, but I've seen a photo of him and he looks a right shifty sort! Oh well they say love is blind don't they?'

'They certainly do. Still, not your problem is it Sal. If she wants to get involved with someone a bit dodgy then that's her lookout. He's not a local bloke is he?'

'No he lives somewhere in Kent I think. They only see each other a couple of times a week. Reckons work commitments make it difficult to see her more often. I think he's an estate agent or something – which explains a lot! I thought it might have been because he was married or living with someone but Karen said he used to be married but they divorced years ago and she's adamant he's not seeing anyone else now, so, what can you do?. Anyway, she's only been seeing him for a few months so hopefully it's not that serious. Although you never can tell with Karen, she does wear her heart on her sleeve!'

'Well all you can do is just be there for her when it all goes tits up I suppose, which you know it's going to' laughed Mike as he started to bound up the stairs, two at a time. 'Right, last one back buys the drinks'

They soon got back to their cabin and by the time they had showered and sorted out something to wear, they were both more than ready to get to the bar.

Chapter 4

The place they had chosen to have their pre-dinner drinks in was The Artemis Bar. This was on the same deck as the dining room they wanted to eat in so they wouldn't have too far to go for dinner. The Artemis was spacious, but cosy, with the bar in the centre of the room and tables and big comfy chairs all around it. Cushioned bar stools stood around the bar and it was there that Mike and Sally decided to sit. They had no sooner taken a seat when the barman, whose name was Jasper, appeared to take their order.

Just as Mike had ordered Gin and Tonics for both him and Sally, he got a tap on the back from a tall, dark haired bloke who had his arm round a petit but curvy, Barbie lookalike.

'Hello Mike' said the man, who looked somewhat familiar to Sally. 'Remember me? Simon from the gents when we were getting on. You told us to meet you here'

'Ahh. Simon, sorry couldn't remember your name for toffee. How are you mate? See you managed to get on alright. This is my wife, Sally and obviously you remembered my name!'

'Absolutely. I'm pretty good at names, which comes in handy in my line of work! Lovely to meet you Sally. This is my wife Candy. Well her actual name is Candice but I like to call her Candy because she's so sweet'

Candy, the blonde Barbie lookalike who was hanging off his arm, gave a little giggle.

'Oh, what is he like? He always introduces me to people like that. I really don't deserve him, do I?'

Sally felt an overwhelming urge to throw up.

'We call her Candy because she's so sweet!!' muttered Sally under her breath. 'What a twat!'

After the initial rush of walking around the ship and seeing it in all its grandeur, Sally was now feeling slightly deflated at the thought of spending an evening in the company of this complete knob head and his dopey wife, especially when she had been looking forward to exploring the ship and having a quite meal on their own.

Mike bought Simon and Candice a drink and they moved over to one of the tables. They all commented on how impressed they were with the ship so far and what prompted them to take the plunge and book a cruise.

'Simon planned the cruise for me as a surprise, didn't you sweetie?' said Candice, snuggling up to her husband like a pet dog.

'Well, I got a rather large bonus this year so thought I would splash out on something different. We tend to go to the Caribbean and US quite a lot so I decided to surprise Candy with a relaxing cruse round the Med. She gets quite exhausted and stressed out sometimes in her job, so she really needs this break'

'Oh what sort of work do you do then Candice?' asked Mike

'I work in retail and, as Simon said, it can get quite full on and stressful so I was over the moon when he booked this for me. What about you two?'

'OK' thought Sally, while Mike proceeded to fill them both in on where him and Sally lived and what they did for a living, 'checkout girl in Tesco's then. Must be really stressful!'

'So Simon, what is it that you do for a living exactly?' said Sally, who really wasn't in the slightest bit interested in actually knowing but thought she'd better make an effort to try and join in, if only for Mike's sake and the fact that she could see that Simon was dying for someone to ask him what he did.

'Oh didn't I say, Hun? It's nothing exciting, I'm just an estate agent'

'And a very successful one' piped up Candice. 'He doesn't like bragging, but he was in the top 5 sellers in the whole country, wasn't you sweetheart?'

'Yes I was' agreed Simon, 'and I was number one in our branch in Sittingbourne in Kent this year, hence the bonus. But as Candy said I don't like bragging about it too much but sometimes it's good to let people know that you're a player as you never know who you're talking to, do you?'

And then it hit her exactly where she recognised him from. This smarmy estate agent, sitting here with his bimbo wife, was none other than her best friend Karen's boyfriend. She should have recognised him straight away with his dark, almost black hair and olive skin, which he took from his mother who was Spanish. She'd seen a photo of him before that Karen had shown him, where the two of them were gazing longingly at each other, pretty much how him and Candice were looking at each other now.

'No you're absolutely right about that, Simon. You really never know who you're talking to do you!'

Sally tried to catch Mike's eye to let him know something was up, but he had launched into a conversation with Mr Smarmy about house prices and Candice was just sitting there giving her husband puppy dog eyes.

'So how long have you two been married?' asked Sally, determined to arm herself with as much information as possible for when she spoke to Karen to let her know what a bastard her boyfriend really was.

'Oh we only got married in June' gushed Candice, holding onto Simon's arm for all it was worth. 'We went to Spain for the wedding because Simon's Mum and Dad live there. It was amazing, wasn't it Simon? The ceremony was on the beach and we had the party afterwards at a fabulous hotel overlooking the bay. Best day of our lives wasn't it Babe?'

'Absolutely darling. I'd do it all over again in a heartbeat' said Simon kissing his wife on the head.

Sally thought back and remembered that it was around June that Simon had told Karen he had to go to a funeral as his Mum's sister had died. He said that he would have taken her with him but all the family would be there and it wouldn't be fair on her to meet them at such a sad time. But he did promise her that he would take her in happier circumstances. Obviously that never happened as he hadn't been to his Aunt's funeral at all, the bastard had been getting married!

She desperately tried to catch Mike's attention so she could let him know exactly who Simon was but unfortunately he was now engrossed in a conversation with him about bloody football and Candice was still hanging onto Simon's arm, pretending to look interested in the future of some Russian football manager who got caught with his fingers in the till!!

All Sally wanted to do was go back to the room and message Karen. But then thinking about it, would she really want to know that her "doting" boyfriend was actually cruising around the Med, happily married to a Barbie lookalike! It was something that Sally needed to speak to Mike about and she wanted to do it now!

Unfortunately, Mike had other ideas!

'Why don't we all share a table for dinner seeing as it's our first night and we don't know anyone'

'Sounds like a fabulous idea' gushed smarmy Simon. 'That OK with you two lovely ladies?'

'Well to be honest' said Sally in her best "pretending to be ill voice". 'I don't actually feel that great. I've got a banging headache and I feel more than a little bit sick. I think I may go back to the cabin and have a lie down. I can always get some room service later, if I feel a bit better. I don't want to spoil your evening by being ill so you three go ahead and eat without me" said Sally knowing full well that Mike wouldn't dare go off without her.

'Oh Sal, why didn't you say earlier that you felt rough, I wouldn't have dragged you out if I'd have known' said Mike looking concerned. 'Actually you do look a bit pale. Perhaps we'd better leave this until another night. I'm really sorry about this Simon but I'm going to have to go back with Sally, I can't leave her to be ill on her own'

'No, that's absolutely fine. We can arrange to have dinner another night. It's not like we're going anywhere is it? We're all in this boat together!'

Simon laughed at his little joke and Candice followed suit.

'Oh Simon you are so funny. Such a shame you feel rough Sally, we could have had a real laugh tonight' said Candice, still laughing at Simon's joke. 'I think we're all going to get on like a house on fire'.

'As long as it's not a ship on fire' snorted Simon as he and Candice started laughing their heads off.

'Right, I really do need to get back to the cabin now' said Sally grabbing hold of Mike's arm and steering him away from the cackling duo at the bar.

They could still hear them laughing as Sally almost dragged Mike along the corridor.

'Quick, if we get the lift up to deck 11 just along here, we can go and have a meal at the Dionyssis Grill Room. It looked really nice in there and you don't have to book. I could just eat a nice steak, I'm starving'

'Hang on a minute.' Mike stopped dead in his tracks and looked at Sally. 'Why are we going to the Grill Room? A minute ago we were going back to the cabin because you were about to chuck up everywhere and now you want to go and eat steak. What's going on Sal?'

'OK, I know it sounds a bit mental but I had to get out of there and away from them two. You're not going to believe who your new little friend is?'

'Oh here we go, he's not someone famous for being in Big Brother or something is he?' said Mike starting to slowly walk towards the lift again.

'No such luck. He's only Karen's creepy boyfriend isn't he! I knew there was something dodgy about him but I didn't know that he was married. What a bastard!

They managed to get a table for two in the Dionyssis Grill, right by the window, and ordered a bottle of Rioja while they looked through the menu. It was a very comprehensive menu and had a variety of steaks with different sauces, grilled fish and shellfish, ribs, chops and massive mixed grills.

'So, what do you think?' asked Sally taking a large glug of the wine that had just been poured for her.

'Well, to be honest, I can't make my mind up between the T-bone steak and the mixed grill, they both look amazing. But, saying that, so does the surf and turf and I haven't had that in years.'

'Not the bloody food you dope, what do you think I should do about Simon? Do you think I should tell Karen that we're sailing round the Med with her boyfriend and his new wife or just let it go and let her find out the hard way? Or should I confront Simon and let him know his little game is up?'

'Difficult one that' said Mike in between mouthfuls of bread roll. 'On the one hand it's not really your place to grass Simon up to Karen. She's a big girl now and if she's picked a wrong- un then that's not really your problem. But, saying that, if I was in her shoes, I'd hate to think that my best friend knew my boyfriend was happily married and hadn't told me. I think it's going to have to be your call on this one. Why don't you sleep on it and decide what to do tomorrow. Now, what are you having off this menu, I don't know about you but I'm bloody starving?'

They both had a lovely evening in the restaurant and then made their way back to the cabin for a quick drink. They did think about popping back into the bar for a nightcap, but the thought of bumping into Simon and Candice made them think otherwise, so they decided to have a glass or two of the wine that they had bought with them, on their balcony instead.

Chapter 5

Sally didn't sleep well that night as she kept going over in her head what she was or wasn't going to tell Karen about her shit of a boyfriend. In the end she decided that there was nothing she could do while they were all in the middle of the Med so she would wait until she got home and then go and see her friend face to face with the news that her boyfriend was in fact happily married. With that decided, she finally fell into a deep sleep, waking only when she heard Mike opening the balcony door to take his mug of tea outside.

'I hope you made me one of those' muttered Sally just before Mike pulled the balcony door shut.

'Sorry love, I thought you were asleep. Here, have this and I'll make another one, the water's still hot. I didn't want to wake you as you seemed to be tossing and turning a lot last night. Still mulling over what to do about Karen's shitty boyfriend?'

'Yeah, I must admit I didn't sleep that well' said Sally sitting up in bed to take the mug of tea that Mike had just made. 'But, I have decided not to do anything until we get home. There's no point in upsetting Karen when I'm so far away and to be fair, it would be pretty horrible of me to tell her on the phone or by e-mail anyway. I'm sure another couple of weeks isn't going to make much difference!'

'No I'm sure you're right' agreed Mike. 'Now get out of that bed and put something on. I've ordered room service breakfast so we can watch the ship coming into Kefalonia from the comfort of our balcony and it will be here any minute'

As if on cue, a knock on the door signalled the arrival of their breakfast and they proceeded to tuck into a selection of fruits with Greek yoghurt, freshly cooked Danish pastries, croissants and a large pot of steaming hot coffee whilst watching the flickering lights of Argostoli get nearer. Just as they had finished the last pastry, the Grecian Princess berthed on the quayside of their first destination.

By the time they had showered, got dressed and made their way down to the allocated deck to disembark, it was getting on for 9.30 and the sun was doing its best impression of a blow torch. They made their way down the gangplank with, what seemed like the rest of the ship, and hailed one of the many taxis that were waiting by the quayside.

They had decided not to pre-book any of the tours on offer and just see what took their fancy on the day. It just so happened that they had been to Kefalonia a few years back. It had only been for a week and they had always hankered to go back there one day and see the places they didn't get to see before. One of the places that they had really wanted to visit was Skala, and it was there that the taxi was now heading to.

The journey was around 45 mins but the taxi was comfortable and air conditioned and, as they were in no particular rush, they just sat back and enjoyed the scenery.

'Do you know what, I'd almost forgotten how beautiful this place is' sighed Sally, her head pressed against the window, soaking up the breath taking views of the sea from where they were heading, high up in the pine forests.

'You have been to Kefalonia before, Kyria?' asked the taxi driver who had introduced himself earlier as Yianni.

'Yes we have Yianni, but a long time ago. Although I must admit, it doesn't seem to have changed much. Have the problems that Greece has been having affected you at all?'

'No, not really, we carry on as normal here. It doesn't really affect the islands, it is Athens that has suffered the most. If you go there you will see many peoples are now in the poverty, where once they had good job and plenty of foods to eat. It is so sad to see. We Greeks are very proud peoples and do not like to ask for help. If your brother, father or neighbour is having problems you will help them but if you have nothing yourself, then how can you do this? It is difficult, but enough of our troubles Kyria, you are here on this beautiful island of mine to enjoy yourselves and be happy, no?'

'Oh yes, we certainly are' sighed Sally feeling more relaxed than she had in ages.

The drive to Skala was very picturesque and Mike and Sally were almost sad to get out of the taxi when they finally got there. But the lure of a cold beer and the chance to jump in the sea was too much, so they paid Yianni, booked him to come and pick them back up at around 3 o'clock to take them back to the ship, and made their way to the nearest bar.

By now the heat was searing and the two ice cold glasses of Mythos went down extremely well. They decided they would have a walk around the town first and then have a couple of hours on the beach and a spot of lunch before meeting Yianni in the town square to get the taxi back to the ship.

Skala wasn't a big town but it had a good selection of bars, tavernas and little shops and a quaint town square that was ringed by beautiful pine trees, making it a lovely cool place to socialise, as was evident in the small groups of elderly Greek men all sitting around, chatting and putting the world to rights. They even saw one old man sitting under the trees sharing his lunch with a goat! It was all very traditional and not at all built up or commercialised, which pleased both Mike and Sally who hated loud, brash resorts full of karaoke and burger bars. After looking in one or two gift shops and buying the obligatory fridge magnet and key ring, they decided that it was too hot to be walking about and headed down to the beach. They chose a couple of sun beds in front of a taverna so that they wouldn't have far to walk for a drink or something to eat, and got down to the serious business of sunbathing.

After soaking up some rays and then having a swim in the warm shallow waters of the Ionian Sea, they had built up quite an appetite, especially when the smell of barbequed food started wafting across from the taverna opposite. Once they had dried off they wandered over to where the mouth-watering smells were coming from and found a table just a stones' throw from the shoreline.

Costas was a typical Greek taverna, with blue and white furniture and Greek music playing softly in the background. A cheerful looking, well rounded man, who they presumed was Costas, came out to welcome them and hand out menus.

'Oh this is the life' said Mike as they sat looking out over the sea. 'I actually wouldn't mind coming here for a week or so, it's a really lovely place, so relaxing and some lovely places to eat by the looks of it'

'Yeah, perhaps we could look to come for a week or two next June if we've nothing else booked. There's a really nice hotel that we passed earlier on. We could pop in there on the way back and get some details. Now, what shall we order, it all looks so nice I can't decide. What about doing what the Greeks do and ordering a few bits and just sharing?'

So that's what they did and when their food arrived it looked amazing. There was some tzatziki with pitta bread, a large Greek salad, a plate of calamari and a portion of the famous Kefalonian meat pie with some Greek roast potatoes on the side. Mike and Sally tucked into the food, washing it down with a carafe of village red wine.

'That was delicious' said Sally patting her tummy. 'I couldn't eat another thing, in fact I think I'll pass on dinner tonight'

'Yeah right' laughed Mike. 'I'll believe that when I see it. I bet you buy a piece of baklava from that bakery across the road to take back with you to eat on the balcony later on'

'Oh, I forgot about the bakery. Perhaps I should just get a couple of bits and put them in the fridge for tomorrow!'

They settled up with Costas, had a walk back into the town to pick up some details from the hotel that they had seen, then bought some baklava from the bakery. By the time they got back to the square, Yianni was pulling up in his taxi. They both got in the car, grateful for the air conditioning, and sat mostly in companionable silence watching the ever changing views go past.

The journey back didn't seem to take so long and in no time at all they could see the ship, in all her magnificence, sitting there waiting for them. They boarded with plenty of time to spare and went straight back to their cabin to have a shower, ready to go out for dinner later that evening. As they had a while before they had to start getting dressed, they sat on the balcony for a couple of hours reading and having a glass or two of chilled wine. They watched the ship silently slip out of Argostoli harbour and into open seas before going back inside and getting changed for dinner.

That evening, they decided to eat in the buffet as, after the enormous lunch they had eaten in Skala, they didn't feel that hungry. Until they saw the food that is. Considering that earlier she thought she would pass on dinner, Sally managed to consume a whole plateful of food and still go back for dessert. Mike, on the other hand, just had a bowl of soup, and then some lasagne with chips and then a large bowl of rice pudding!

'So much for taking it easy tonight then' laughed Sally when she saw the amount of food Mike had consumed. 'What's with the rice pudding then? I didn't even know you liked the stuff.'

'I don't normally. But I've had a craving for it after that bloke on the forum keeps going on about it.'

'What bloke on the forum?' asked Sally, waving the waiter over for some coffee.

'Rick Hoben, the guy who seems to run most of the cruise forums. I joined them all when we first had the idea of going on a cruise. I did send them to you as well!'

'Oh right, I know who you mean now. Doesn't he go on about three cruises a year with his wife, oh, what's her name?'

'That's the one' said Mike 'His wife is called Kaz, if I'm not mistaken. Well, every time he goes on a cruise he makes a bee line for the rice pudding and since I saw a picture of it that he posted, I've fancied it and it's not that bad! Actually, I've got a feeling they might even be on this cruise. I might have a look on-line when we get back to the cabin. If they are, we should go and introduce ourselves to him and his wife.'

'Oh definitely' agreed Sally 'I have read a few of his posts and he sounds a right character. Mike, surely you're not going to have another bowl of it, you'll explode!'

'I need building up' explained Mike.

'God, I wish I could eat like you and not put on any weight' sighed Sally. 'I've only got to look at a cake and I put on half a stone.'

'I know, but you've done so well losing all that weight Sal, I'm really proud of you. Not that you needed to lose weight in the first place. It's not like you were that fat. I'm digging myself into a hole now aren't I?'

'Yep, I'd give up while the going's good if I were you! That was bloody hard work losing all the weight that I did and I won't be happy if I put it all back on again. Still a couple of weeks back at the slimming club when we get home will soon shift anything that I put on and, at the end of the day, I'm on holiday so, sod the diet! Right I don't know about you but I'm absolutely knackered, must be all that sea air. Shall we go and have a nightcap on the balcony again? Don't forget we've still got that baklava to eat, it won't last until tomorrow'

And with that they made their way back to their cabin for a mug of coffee and slice of baklava. Mike looked on-line and confirmed that Rick and Kaz were indeed on the same ship. He put a quick post on one of the forums saying he would try and find him to buy him a drink and then they both retired for the night.

Chapter 6

The next day dawned just as glorious as the previous. This was to be a day at sea and a chance to catch up on getting a tan. That evening was the first of the ships formal nights, giving everyone a chance to dress up in their evening gowns and dinner suits. Sally was really looking forward to getting glammed up and having a chance to show off her new slim figure, but she also wanted a bit of tan to go with it, so they both spent the whole day up on deck laying in the sun, reading and swimming, though obviously not all at the same time!

They went back to their cabin around 4.30, showered and had half an hour on the balcony with the now obligatory glass of wine before getting into their glad rags.

Sally had treated herself to a beautiful floor length dress from a little, but extremely expensive, boutique that had recently opened in Romford. It was black, flecked with silver and had a cowl neck and flowing sleeves. It fitted perfectly and was clingy enough to show off her curves but not too much as to be tight. Sally complimented the dress by adding a matching diamanté necklace, bracelet and earrings and donning a pair of sparkly, skyscraper heels that she could hardly walk in. By the time she had finished primping and preening it was time to leave. Mike on the other hand managed to get into his black tuxedo, complete with azure blue bow tie and matching cummerbund, in under 10 minutes. Then, with a smidgeon of gel in his short, spikey hair and a splash of aftershave, he was ready. They both looked amazing and felt like a million dollars as they walked down the corridor.

When they reached the main atrium, it was a mass of dinner suits and glittery dresses, high heeled shoes and jewellery. Waiters were walking round handing out glasses of champagne and trays of delicate hors d'oeuvres and the noise of everyone chatting at the same time was deafening. As they were a few minutes early, they had their picture taken on the stairs of the Atrium by the professional photographer and then stood drinking champagne and admiring all the finery until the Captain appeared on the stairs with his staff to make a speech. After a good 15 minutes of standing listening to him thank all his staff for helping to make the cruise such a success, Sally's feet were killing her. It was the first time she had worn high heels in years and she was beginning to wish she hadn't. She breathed a sigh of relief when the Captain finally finished, everyone gave him a round of applause and they started to make their way to one of the 2 dining rooms that were hosting that night's gala dinner.

As they entered the dining room they were asked whether they would like a table for two or if they would like to share a table. As the only table for two available was right next to the kitchen, they decided to take the plunge and share a table. At the end of the day, meeting new people was all part of the holiday and, worst case scenario they were lumbered with a bunch of dickheads, they wouldn't need to sit with them again for the rest of the cruise.

The table that they were shown to was laid for 8 but so far only one couple was seated. They were a couple around the same ages as Sally and Mike, late 40s, early 50s and looked quite normal. After some of the people they had met so far this was a massive relief. The couple introduced themselves as Richard and Hannah Barnes and Sally and Mike sat down next to them and introduced themselves. Richard and Mike seemed to get on immediately, due mostly to their love of football but Hannah was a little bit more hard work. She was very quiet and Sally found it very hard to get a conversation out of her. Richard told them that it was Hannah's first cruise and that he had badgered her to go on one ever since he had known her. He had been on a few cruises in his youth with his parents and he always loved them.

Hannah admitted that it was all very nice and yes she was enjoying her holiday but she did miss her cat. Talking about the cat, whose name was Titchmarsh (and yes, you guessed, her other love was gardening!) was the only time she seemed at all animated. The rest of the time she seemed to find it hard to say anything at all and to be fair, Sally couldn't find the enthusiasm to carry on trying! In fact she was quite glad when the waiter brought over another couple to their table. But unfortunately her relief quickly turned to horror when the couple in question turned out to be no other than Prudence and her lapdog husband George.

'Oh how lovely' trilled Prudence. 'We meet again. It's Jenny and Dick isn't it?'

'No, actually its Sally and Mike, but near enough! It's lovely to see you both again too. Sally was only saying this afternoon that she wondered if we would bump into you again, didn't you Sal?'

Sally kicked Mike under the table and gave him a withering look 'Absolutely Prudence, like Mike said, it's great to see you again. I hope you've been enjoying yourselves. By the way, this is Richard and Hannah. It's Hannah's first cruise as well so I'm sure she would benefit from your wealth of experience and would love to hear about all the cruises that you and George have been on!'

'Touché' thought Sally as Prudence turned to Hannah and started to regale her with stories of her many cruises. 'Good luck with that friendship – Mrs Bouquet!'

The next addition to the party was seated next to Sally and introduced himself as Anton Russell. He was a 60 something, single gay man whose flamboyant mannerisms made Dale Winton look positively butch and Sally adored him on sight. Sally had a lot of gay friends at home and Mike always said that her "gaydar" never let her down, especially when she was on holiday.

Sally and Anton hit it off immediately and started chatting away as if they had known each other all their lives. They were still talking when the final seat on the table was taken by a rather glamorous lady, who introduced herself as Valerie Landsdown. Valerie was quite petit and dressed immaculately. Her chestnut brown hair was swept up in a chignon, held in place by a very sparkly diamanté clip and her nails were beautifully manicured. When she spoke, she had an unexpected broad Yorkshire accent and Sally was convinced she recognised the voice although she was certain that she had never met the lady sitting opposite her now.

Once everyone had been seated at the table, waiters appeared as if by magic and took their orders. It was a 5 course gala meal and Sally had been looking forward to it all day. The menu didn't disappoint at all, and both Sally and Mike savoured the fine food and wine and enjoyed the conversation that flowed around the table. Course after course of mouth-watering delights such as lobster served three ways, roasted quail, haunch of venison with a port sauce and mini strawberry pavlovas served in spun sugar baskets were brought out by a team of immaculate waiters and served up to the hordes of hungry passengers.

The last course of a cheeseboard, complete with glass of port, finally appeared much to the relief of most people who were full to bursting point by this time.

'Blimey, that's well and truly undone all my hard work at "Slim 2 Win". I'd better get back there pretty sharpish when we get home or I'll end up a right lard arse' said Sally, to Mike, holding her belly as if it was going to explode.

'That's it!' cried Valerie pointing to Sally, 'I knew I'd seen you somewhere before. You went to Jenny Jarvis's "Slim 2 Win" class for a few weeks in Norfolk didn't you?'

'Yes, I did' said Sally, desperately trying to remember if she'd seen Valerie there, 'but I really don't remember you, I'm sorry. The only Valerie I remember there was a really large lady who used to go with her husband Brian, a bit of a pervert from what I remember'

Valerie was nodding at Sally grinning, 'Aye, that'll be me then'.

'No way, it can't be. Wow, you look amazing. You must have lost shedloads of weight. Oh, and Brian, is he not with you?'

Sally blushed after remembering she'd just called him a pervert!

'No, I got rid of him and aye, you were right lass, he were a pervert. A big, fat slob of a pervert and I still can't believe I stayed with him for that long. Anyway, once I got rid of him, I decided to live my life again. I found that I didn't need to have a food substitute anymore as I were happier than I had been in ages and once the weight started coming off, I made inroads on the image'

'Well you look stunning. Talk about an advert for "Slim 2 Win", I bet Jenny was really proud of you'

'Ah, thanks love, yes our Jenny were right proud. I actually got Slimmer of the Month twice in class and won the national Slimmer of the Year award just before I came away. That were brilliant. Had a night in a posh hotel in London and was presented the award by that woman who does morning telly. When I think back to how I was this time last year, I sometimes have to pinch myself to make sure it's real!'

'My dear Valerie that's amazing, what an achievement. But surely that's not a Norfolk accent you have though?' said Anton.

'No, I'm a Yorkshire lass, originally from just outside Leeds but I relocated to Norfolk about 5 years ago'.

'Oh right' said Anton. 'That makes much more sense. So what about you Sally? Do you hail from Norfolk? Only you sound extremely "Essex", if you don't mind me saying!'

'Oh no, me and Mike both come from Essex. Hornchurch actually, which is the posh part' laughed Sally. 'Mike's Dad lives in Norfolk, has done for a few years now, and we stayed with him for a few weeks earlier in the year after he had a heart attack. I go to the "Slim 2 Win" slimming club in Hornchurch and I didn't want to miss my weigh-ins so I went for a few weeks to one of the classes in Norfolk. That's how I met Valerie and, as I said, she's half the size of when I saw her last'.

'Aye, but saying that Sally' interjected Valerie, 'you must have lost a good couple of stone yourself since I last saw you, so I really can't take all the praise'

'Thanks Valerie. Yeah, I lost just over 3 stone but, to be fair, quite a bit of that was due to stress after I lost my Mum suddenly in May. But I will be going back to my class in Hornchurch after this as I've got a feeling I may put on a few pounds!'

'Oh my God you poor things' exclaimed Anton. 'You and Mike really have had a year of it haven't you? No wonder you booked a cruise. I would image that you needed holiday after a year like that'

'No, it hasn't been one of our better years' agreed Mike. 'And we only thought about going on a cruise because I had been made redundant! Luckily I found another job pretty much straight away so it wasn't too much of a problem, but after that it just seemed to be one thing after another. Still, in the words of Jazz, the only way is up!'

'It's Yazz' spluttered Sally as she nearly choked on her wine.

'What is?' said Mike, totally bewildered.

'It's Yazz that sang "the only way is up", not Jazz you donut!'

The whole table, Hannah included, erupted into laughter as the first evening with new found friends drew to a close.

On their way back to the cabin, both Sally and Mike were buzzing and both agreed that this had been the best night of their holiday so far. Sally was still singing the Yazz classic until Mike finally turned off the light and they fell into a deep, alcohol fuelled sleep.

Chapter 7

The next day seemed even hotter than the day before and, with the mother of all headaches due to the copious amounts of booze she had downed the night before, Sally decided that she would stay on board ship. The port of call for that day was Piraeus and Sally was in no fit state to walk around museums, shops or churches. In fact it was as much as she could do to get dressed and go to breakfast. Mike on the other hand was wide awake and had a positive spring to his step.

'Why don't you ever suffer with hangovers?' moaned Sally as she sat at the breakfast table contemplating whether a fry up would be a good idea or not.

'Maybe it's because I don't drink as much as you!'

'I didn't drink that much' protested Sally, grabbing the nearest waiter who was walking round with a jug of hot coffee.

'Really! I think you'll find you did. Champagne before the meal, wine with the meal, port with cheese, liqueurs with coffee and then shots of God knows what up at the bar with Anton and Valerie'

'Oops, I forgot about that. Blimey no wonder my head's banging!'

'Well, you are on your holidays, if you can't do it then when can you?' Mike laughed as he tucked into his full English with gusto.

They had just finished their breakfast when Richard came bounding over to their table.

'Hello Mate' said Mike to his new found buddy. 'How's your head this morning? Poor old Sal here has got the hangover from hell, even though she reckons she didn't drink that much'.

'No, I'm absolutely fine' said Richard looking even more alert than Mike, if that was even possible! 'But I must admit if I'd have drunk half of what you did last night Sally, I think I'd be in the hospital wing by now'.

'Oh very funny Richard, make me out to be a right lush why don't you? I notice your wife was putting them away last night as well'

'Don't I know it, I've left her in bed as she was chucking up half the night. She's blaming it on the seafood and reckons she was mainly drinking tonic water, but I think you're right, she was necking the wine a bit last night. Anyway, I'm glad I found you both. I wondered if you fancied a wander round Piraeus, there's supposed to be a brilliant museum there. The Hellenic Maritime Museum I think it's called, that's if you're into boats and stuff? I was going to go with Hannah but obviously she's in no state to go now'

'I wouldn't mind seeing that actually' enthused Mike. 'I was reading about it in the ship's magazine, it looks really interesting. Do you fancy it Sal or would you rather walk round the shops?'

'To be quite honest, Babe, I think I'd rather spend the day on a sunbed with my Kindle but you two go ahead and explore and do some men things, just remember to bring me back a fridge magnet!'

'Right then, I'll just pop back to the cabin and get my wallet and camera. Now are you sure you don't mind, I hate the thought of you being on here on your own'

'Mike, I'm hardly on my own, there's 3,000 people on here' laughed Sally. 'But no, I'll be fine. I might even go mad and have a couple of treatments at the Spa. If I'm not in the cabin when you get back, just text me in case I'm still deck asleep on a sunbed somewhere. Have a lovely time and take lots of photos!'

Once Mike and Richard left to go on their shore excursion, Sally had yet another cup of coffee then wandered back to the cabin to get changed into her bikini. After a couple of hours of soaking up the sun and reading a bit more of the latest Jack Reacher novel, she decided that, although her headache had all but gone, she'd had enough sun for one day and decided to cover up and go and explore the ship.

She hadn't got very far when she bumped into Anton, who had obviously had the same idea as her.

'Hello my gorgeous girl, what on earth are you doing out here on your own wandering round the ship and where is that husband of yours? Surely you haven't been abandoned?'

'No, not yet' laughed Sally. 'He's gone off to some maritime museum with Mike but I preferred to stay on board and do a bit of exploring. What about you? Not going off on some excursion?'

'Eugh, how ghastly. I couldn't think of anything more boring. I think you were very wise to stay on board. No, I couldn't be bothered to walk around in this heat. I've had a swim and a bit of sun but now I fancy having a look round. Now what sort of mischief do you think we could get up to while we're unattended?'

'Well I think before we do anything we should go to the nearest bar for a pre-lunch gin and tonic and plan the rest of our day.'

'Sounds perfect my dear, lead the way.'

They trotted off together arm in arm and ended up in the Medusa Bar which was right at the back of the ship on the top deck. It had magnificent 360 degree views all over the ship and out to sea and also served a splendid G and T!

After being revitalised by a couple of large Bombay Sapphires, Sally and Anton decided to have a walk around the ship and see what was on offer. As it happened there was a lot more than they had bargained for!

They left the bar and started off down a couple of flights of stairs. The first corridor they came to lead to the Spa deck, passing through where the suites were situated. Sally wanted to have a look at the Spa area and get a treatment brochure, so that's where they made their way towards. As they walked through the corridor, Sally stopped dead.

'Can you hear that' she said, craning her head to the nearest door.

'No, what?' said Anton, straining to listen. 'Can't hear a thing'

'There it is again, someone is crying for help. I'm sure it's coming from that door there'.

They both put their ears to the door and, sure enough, a woman's voice could be heard, pleading for help.

'Told you' said Sally, looking around for someone to open the door. 'Right nip through there Anton and find a steward or a cleaner to get this door open'

Off he went through the door further down, marked Staff, to find someone, while Sally shouted through the door.

'It's OK we're getting someone to open the door to help you, they won't be a minute'

Anton soon came back with a cleaner hot on his heels who swiped his card to open the door and then left just as quickly to go back to the staff area. Sally wasn't sure what she expected to see once the door was opened but she certainly didn't expect to see Prudence and her lapdog husband George dressed up in bondage gear!

Prudence was wearing leather underwear that certainly didn't leave much to the imagination, and a dog collar, complete with spikes and a bizarre sparkly name tag!! She was cuffed to the bed with black rubber handcuffs and George, complete with leather thong, nipple clamps and gimp mask, lay slumped on the floor. It certainly was a sight for sore eyes and Sally thought maybe they had wandered into some parallel universe by mistake!

Prudence looked mortified that it was Sally and Anton that had found them dressed like that and she averted her eyes so she didn't have to see the look of amusement on their faces.

'It's George' she cried, 'he's diabetic and I think his sugar levels have dropped. You must try and get me off here, I need to get some sugar into him before he goes into a hypo. The key to the padlock is over there by the television. Please hurry before we're too late'

Anton grabbed the key and unlocked the handcuffs that were holding Prudence captive. She tumbled off the bed, opened the fridge and took out a carton of fruit juice. Kneeling on the floor beside him, Prudence carefully dripped juice into George's mouth. After what seemed like ages, but was most probably only seconds, a very groggy George began to come round.

'Do you want me to call the ship's doctor or something' asked Sally, who, although concerned about George, was also starting to feel an uncontrollable urge to giggle build up inside her.

'No it's fine, George will be OK now' said Prudence, who was frantically trying to cover herself up with a bath robe. 'I'll call room service and get him something to eat and it will be alright. In fact you can both go now. Thank you for helping me out but I really think we need to be on our own now.'

George was now fully awake and starting to sit up.

'Hello my beauty' slurred George still a bit woozy. 'Have you come to join in the fun?'

'No she hasn't' cried Prudence. 'In fact they were just leaving, weren't you?'

Prudence almost pushed them out of the door but before she closed it she whispered to Sally and Anton.

'I know what this looks like and I can't dress it up to be something it isn't, but please, I beg of you, don't tell anyone else about this. Can it be our little secret?'

'Oh I'm sure we can keep it between us, can't we Sally? If I was you I would get back to George and get some clothes on him before he catches pneumonia. Will we see you at dinner?'

Prudence muttered something and shut the door firmly behind her.

Both Sally and Anton looked at each other and collapsed laughing.

'Bloody hell, what on earth was going on there?' said Sally, tears rolling down her face as she tried to stop laughing. 'There she is, the snooty cow, making out she's better than everyone else and all the time her and her seemingly placid husband are into the old S & M scene. Well, who would have thought it?'

'I know' laughed Anton. 'Of all the people, they would have been the last ones you would have suspected. And what about old George. They say the quiet ones are the worst, but really, did you see what the silly old fool looked like with his gimp mask on? I don't know about you but I really think I need another drink after experiencing that'

They were still laughing when they got back to the bar and ordered up another couple of large G and T's.

Chapter 8

After having a spot of lunch and then a wander over to the Spa to pick up the details that they were supposed to get earlier before they were interrupted, they sat in the atrium with a coffee, watching all the old folk ballroom dancing while they waited for Mike and Richard to come back on board.

'So then my dear, I've been dying to ask, what's the story behind Valerie's ex-husband? I heard you both call him a pervert and I didn't like to ask at the dinner table last night. But, after the day we've had I think you need to spill!'

'Well' said Sally in her best conspiratory voice. 'By all accounts, Valerie and Brian had to move away from their native Yorkshire after Brian, who had always fancied himself as a bit of a ladies man, went and touched up the boss's niece where he worked. I think it could have gone a lot further if he hadn't been disturbed. As it was, he was beaten up quite badly by the girl's fiancée and her dad, and was then told to get out of town or else. I only met him a couple of times but he was really slimy. A bit fat lump who used to letch after anything in a skirt. We all used to feel really sorry for Valerie having to put up with a pig like that. Obviously he never learnt his lesson as she finally kicked him out. Best thing she could have done if you ask me. But, enough of Valerie, what about you? What's your story? Do you have a partner or are you single?'

'I did have a partner' said Anton, suddenly looking very serious. 'But unfortunately he died a couple of years ago and I really don't have the inclination or the strength to get involved with anyone else. Kenny was my soulmate and I'm afraid part of me died when he did'

'Oh Anton, I'm so sorry. I really wish I hadn't asked now. Trust me to put my foot in it!'

'No, no Sally that's quite alright. If you'd have asked me a year ago I may have burst into tears but I'm OK talking about him now. It still hurts and I miss him every day but I'm learning to live with it now'

'So, I take it you were with Kenny for a long time then' asked Sally

'Yes, we were together for nearly 30 years. It's ironic really, we were going to have our 30th anniversary on this very ship but he became too ill to go anywhere. Before he passed away, he made me promise that I would do this cruise in memory of him, so that's why I'm on here'

'Oh, that is so sad Anton. What was it, if you don't mind me asking, Cancer?'

'I think I could have handled that better, but no, he was murdered by some little scroat who attacked and raped him on his way home from work one night. He was an actor in the theatre. A proper "luvvie" was my Kenny or Kenneth as he insisted on his fellow thespians calling him. He wasn't in any of the mainstream shows. He did Shakespeare mainly, although he did always hanker after a part in The Rocky Horror Show. Who knows, he may have even done it if he had lived! Anyway, he quite often stayed behind for drinks after a show and this particular night he was a little bit tipsy and decided to walk home instead of getting his normal taxi. It was only a 20 minute walk but that night changed our lives forever'

'Oh my God' exclaimed Sally 'that's horrendous. What happened? Did he get stabbed or something?'

'No, he only had a couple of cuts and bruises. Obviously he was in shock and was distraught about being raped but it wasn't until he had the routine medical that you have after being raped, that we found out he had been infected with the HIV virus. The little shit who infected him knew he was a carrier so when he was finally caught, he was tried and found guilty of attempted murder'.

'Bloody hell, that's unbelievable. How could someone do that?' said Sally stunned by what Anton had just told her. 'I bet it was a relief when he was caught and sentenced?'

'Well yes, it was great that he had been caught and put away, but it didn't alter the fact that he would be out in 5 years but poor Kenny had a life sentence hanging over him. He caught full blown AIDS about 3 or 4 years after the attack and went downhill quite rapidly.

The change in him was heart breaking and to be honest it was a blessed release when he finally took his last breath.

I was tested as soon as Kenny got the diagnosis and luckily it came back negative. We were extremely careful after that and I was tested frequently up until he passed away. I must admit, more than a few times, I wished that I had been infected and that I could have gone with Kenny but I'm over that and now I try to live my life to the full so that I have loads of stuff to tell him when we do finally meet up again.

I do a lot of charity work for the AIDS Foundation now. I gave up an extremely well paid job in the City to look after Kenny in his final months and then, after he passed, I decided that I couldn't go back there and that I would spend my time working at the Foundation. I do get paid for the admin that I do but I also give a lot of time freely. I don't need the money as I had quite a bit put away from the sale of my mother and father's house from when they passed a few years back, and then Kenny left me more than adequately provided for. Mind you I'd give it all back in a heartbeat to have him back again!'

'Wow. That is an amazing story and I'm sure Kenny would be really proud knowing that you are helping others that are going through what he did.'

'Thanks Sally, I appreciate that. You would be surprised at the amount of people that shunned me when they found out what happened, as if I am somehow tainted with the virus myself and when I tell people where I work, you would think it was a leper colony by the looks on their faces!'

'No it doesn't surprise me in the least' said Sally wearily 'there are a lot of bigoted and uneducated people out there. Unfortunately, that's the way of the world nowadays. I think it's rather sad that we've evolved in that way but, what can you do. I'm afraid there will always be people that are not tolerant of others and expect everyone to share their views. It's just a good job that we're not all like that!'

'I couldn't have put that better myself Sal. Now before we sit here and depress ourselves any further, let's go downstairs and meet Mike and Richard because I've just seen them coming alongside the ship and I don't like to worry you but Mike seemed to be carrying an awful lot of bags!'

They downed the last of their coffees and raced downstairs to meet Mike and Richard as they boarded the ship and, sure enough, Mike was laden down with bags and packages. Richard on the other hand had just the one small bag.

'Please tell me that you're carrying some of those bags for Richard?' pleaded Sally as she looked in mock horror at the amount of stuff Mike had carried on with him.

'I tried to stop him Sally but he was like a man possessed. One shop after another. He said it was his way of helping the Greek economy but I just think he's got a serious shopping addiction!' Mike made a face at Richard who was laughing.

'Thanks Mate, you're supposed to be on my side'

'Oh well, as long as you've got something in that lot for me, I'll let you off' said Sally.' Now let's go back to the cabin for a rest before we get ready for dinner. I've got loads to tell you'

They all said their goodbyes, arranging to meet up later in the bar for drinks before dinner, and went off to their respective cabins. On the way there, Sally started telling Mike all about finding George in his gimp mask and Prudence tied up on her bed in leather undies. Mike was genuinely shocked and both of them couldn't stop laughing all the way back to their cabin.

When they got in, Sally pounced on Mike straight away.

'Right, what have you got in all those bags then?'

Mike ceremoniously dumped all his carrier bags on the bed and emptied them one by one. Out came bottles of Retsina, and Ouzo, tubs of feta cheese and olives and boxes of baklava and kafaifi. More bags revealed a selection of the Greek evil eyes and three sets of komboloi (Greek worry beads!). Then there was a Greek flag beach towel, a set of tea towels with Greek dancers and donkeys on them and a t-shirt and some literature from the Maritime Museum.

'Bloody hell Mike, was there really any need for all this stuff? Please tell me we've got some money left after all this?'

'Don't worry babe, it was all really cheap and most of it is for presents anyway'

'Presents for who exactly? Oh yes, that'll be your Mum and Dad and Karen. At this rate I'll be walking round the street handing stuff out to all the neighbours! I think I'd better come ashore with you next time we dock, you really can't be trusted around shops, can you? Now let's get that box of Baklava open!'

Chapter 9

Mike and Sally chilled out for a while on the balcony with a coffee and some Baklava, and then got ready to meet the others in the bar.

Anton was already sitting at the bar, armed with a dubious looking pink cocktail, complete with parasol and sparklers. He jumped up as soon as he saw Sally and Mike coming over.

'Bloody hell Anton that looks a bit gay!' laughed Mike pointing to the cocktail.

'Shhh, keep your voice down. I don't want everyone knowing about my sexuality'

'Really!' said Mike. 'You've got to be the most gayest bloke on this ship. I would imagine everyone knows about your sexuality, unless they're blind'

'Oh no, I really wanted to keep it a secret. I can't believe you think everyone knows. I'm devastated!' Anton buried his head in his arms whilst Mike looked on crestfallen.

'He's having you on Mike' laughed Sally. 'He's gay and proud and doesn't care who knows. Isn't that right Anton?'

Anton jumped up and sat on Mike's lap, flinging his arms around him.

'Of course I am sweetie. Just a shame that you're happily married or I could quite fancy you myself. What do you reckon Mikey? Fancy batting for the other side?'

'Get off me you lunatic, people will start talking!'

Mike was still trying to prise Anton off his lap when a voice behind them piped up.

'Well I'd never have had you down as a poof Mike. Not with an adorable wife like Sally. I'll take her off your hands if you don't want her mate!'

Sally turned round and there was Simon, smug as ever, leering at her.

'What do you say Sal, shall we run away together and leave these two lovebirds alone?'

'Yeah, when hell freezes over' whispered Sally under her breath, looking at him as if he had just crawled out of the woodwork.

'Friend of yours I take it?' said Anton sarcastically, jumping off Mike's lap.

'Oh Simon, hello mate. No it's not what it looks like, honest' laughed Mike. 'This is Anton by the way. Anton this is Simon. We met him and his wife Candice on our first night and, for some unknown reason, we haven't seen them since!'

'Which suits me down to the ground' whispered Sally to Anton, who was glaring at Simon, 'he's a self-centred, two timing, twatt and his wife is brainless bimbo. But apart from that, they're most probably really nice people!'

'Do tell me more sweetie' whispered Anton.

'Well,' said Sally, steering Anton away from the others so she wouldn't be overheard, 'the lovely Simon, who is happily married to Candice, is also seeing my best friend Karen, who is blissfully unaware that he's married, let alone in the middle of the Med on a cruise. He told her that he was on a lads' only golfing trip in Portugal, the lying shit! Obviously he doesn't realise that I know who he is but I'm sick of putting on an act to try and be civil to the bloke, when all I want to do is tell him his fortune.'

'Have you thought about letting your friend that you know what he's up to?'

'See, that's the dilemma I've been facing since I got on here and recognised him. Do I message Karen and tell her or do I wait until we get home and then let her know? I was happy to go along with the latter, as there's nothing she can really do about it whilst we're in the middle of the ocean. But the more I see him, the more I want to bring his perfect little world crashing down!'

'Mm, difficult' mused Anton, 'but I have to admit, if I were Karen, I think I would want to know what the little rat is up to sooner rather than later. What do they say, "hell hath no fury like a woman scorned? I do think that you need to keep up the act of being civil to him though. You don't want him to think that somethings up and spoil the surprise that's coming to him do you? Sal, stop looking at your phone while I'm speaking to you, this is important stuff. Sally, what is it?'

'Oh my God' whispered Sally excitedly to Anton. 'I think this surprise might come sooner than we thought. I've just had a message from Karen. She's taken a few days off and is going to Rhodes with a couple of friends from work and it just so happens to coincide with when we dock there! She's going to come and meet us at the port as we arrive and spend a few hours with us'

'So all we need to do now' said Anton excitedly, 'is make sure that we walk off the ship in Rhodes with Simon and his wife. I say we, because there's no bloody way I'm missing this! Right you'd better start being nice to Simon as we've only got a few days before it all kicks off!'

As the sun started setting over Piraeus and the Grecian Princess slipped effortlessly out into the Mediterranean Sea, Sally began her charm offensive on Simon and the newly arrived Candice who was now doing her usual doting act whilst hanging off her husband's arm.

'Oh hi Candice, sorry I didn't see you there, I was helping Anton out with a bit of man trouble that he's having at the moment. You look amazing tonight, you really must let me know where you get your dresses from they are stunning"

'Oh thanks Sally. I'm not sure where they come from, Simon bought a couple of these dresses for me when we booked the cruise. He's pretty good at knowing what sort of stuff I like.'

'Really, that's amazing. He really does have great taste doesn't he?'

The fact that Sally wouldn't be seen dead in the thigh skimming, cerise pink creation that Candice had on was immaterial. Hopefully she was dim enough not to realise that Sally was actually being sarcastic and not complimentary!

Simon was being his normal slimy self and Sally found it extremely difficult to even speak to him, let alone be nice. Still, if it meant exposing him for what he really was then it was worth it, and it was only for the next couple of days then hopefully they wouldn't have to talk, or even see them again.

While Sally was trying her hardest to make small talk with Simon and Candice, Valerie had turned up with Richard and Hannah in tow.

'I just found these two loitering in atrium' boomed Valerie in her broad Yorkshire accent. 'I thought 'praps it would be nice if we all had our tea together tonight. There's a lovely restaurant on deck 10 that does proper Greek food. It's supposed to be a replica of a taverna in Crete or somewhere. It's called Pandesia and it looks right authentic. The food's supposed to be great too, so who's up for it?'

After Mike had introduce the newcomers to Simon and Candice, all eight of them decided that Pandesia would be a good idea and off they trotted to deck 10.

Valerie was right when she said it was authentic. The restaurant was decorated in blue and white with traditional whitewashed tables and chairs and grapevines hanging overhead, well plastic ones anyway! The floors were done in a cobbled effect and were awash with pots filled with bougainvillea and geraniums. A couple of guys in the corner playing bouzouki and singing traditional Greek songs completed the effect. In fact it was so well done that you could be fooled into thinking that you were actually outside in a taverna and not sitting inside on a ship.

They were all seated straight away and proceeded to order carafes of red and white wine whilst perusing the menus.

In true Greek fashion, they decided to order meze, a selection of dishes to share. The food was plentiful and delicious and they made their way through bowls of houmous, taramasalata and tzatziki served with olives and warm pitta bread. This was followed by calamari, stuffed vine leaves, meatballs, souvlaki, lamb chops, stuffed tomatoes, moussaka and grilled lemon chicken. For those that had room, there were plates of fresh watermelon, figs, baklava and loukomades with honey.

This veritable feast was washed down by coffees, and Ouzo shots for those that were brave enough and everyone agreed that it had been a fabulous meal and well done to Valerie for suggesting it.

Sally and Mike decided that they would wander off to the music bar to relax for an hour and let their dinner go down a bit before going to bed. Richard and Hannah cried off and went back to their cabin as Hannah wasn't feeling so good and Valerie said she had arranged to meet a couple of ladies she had made friends with in the casino. So with Simon, Candice and Anton in tow, they made their way to the bar.

The entertainment for that night was a Michael Bublé tribute which Sally got quite excited about until he started singing. Although he had a good voice, he also had a broad Wolverhampton accent, and singing "I just haven't met YOW yet", didn't quite have the desired effect. But it did give them all a laugh and rounded the evening off perfectly. Sally was having such a good time that she almost forgot that she hated Simon until Anton asked if anyone had seen the real Mr Bublé and Simon laughed and said that it would be his worst nightmare as he was more into rock music. Sally knew full well that he was lying as he had taken Karen to see him for her birthday last month and she had said that he was a big fan of his and had all his albums. It was at this point that Sally decided it was time to draw the evening to a close, so her and Mike made their way back to their cabin to get some sleep.

Chapter 10

The next day was a sea day and after the frivolities of the night before both Sally and Mike decided to have a bit of a lie in. When they finally emerged, they grabbed some breakfast from the buffet and sat round the pool for a couple of hours reading, listening to music and generally just chilling out.

'Oh look there's Roy' said Mike pointing to an elderly gentleman carrying a couple of drinks from the bar.

'Who the hell's Roy?' asked Sally, not recognising the man Mike was pointing to.

'He's our neighbour. They're in the cabin just below us, him and his wife. Haven't got a clue what her name is or what she looks like but I saw him on the balcony the other night when you were getting ready. Well, I actually heard his wife before I saw him. All I could hear was 'Roy, have you seen my slippers?', 'Roy, will you be eating fish tonight?', 'Roy, is it time for a G & T yet?' All I could hear poor old Roy saying was 'Yes dear' and 'No dear'. I just had to have a peak over the balcony to see what he looked like and there he was sitting on his lounger listening to music with his earphones on, so he obviously couldn't hear a word his wife was saying. I just hope he said yes and no in the right places otherwise I think, by the sounds of her, she'd have had his guts for garters!'

'Oh bless him, I'll have a listen next time I'm out on the balcony, see if I can hear her. This Roy didn't see you hanging over the balcony watching him did he? Only I don't want them thinking they've got a couple of weird, peeping toms above them!'

'No, I don't think so' laughed Mike. 'There's only one set of weirdo's on this ship. Talking of which I haven't seen Prudence and George since you paid them a visit!'

'No, I haven't seen them either. Keeping a low profile if you ask me. They must be so embarrassed. I still can't believe what we saw, I keep having flashbacks, which are not pleasant I can assure you!'

'Ergh – too much information! Right, enough talk of weirdo's. Is it time for lunch yet only I'm feeling a bit peckish?'

'Bloody hell Mike, you only had breakfast a couple of hours ago and the size of the fry up you put away should have been enough to see you through the rest of the day. Are you sure you haven't got worms?' laughed Sally.

'More like boa constrictors the way I've been eating since I've been on here. Come on let's go and hit the buffet'

Sally finally relented and they gathered their stuff together and found a table by the window in the buffet restaurant. They took it in turns to go up and get their lunch so that they wouldn't lose the table they had and then grabbed the nearest waiter for a carafe of wine. They chatted about the ship and the next couple of ports of call before the subject turned to Simon.

'Look, I know he's not your favourite person Sal, but I was chatting with him last night and I actually felt quite sorry for him and Candice'.

'Really, why on earth would you feel sorry for those two?' asked Sally, puzzled.

'Well he was saying that he and Candice would love to have children but unfortunately, due to a rare childhood illness that left him infertile, he is unable to have them. I think Candice is slowly getting used to the idea but Simon sounded really upset about it all when he spoke to me'

'You are kidding me? He actually said that?' fumed Sally. 'What a bastard! You do know that he was married before and has 2 grown up sons that live up north. He's never bothered to see them, or contact them since him and their mother split up about 12 years ago so don't ever feel sorry for that lying, cheating piece of shite!'

'No way. He's already got kids of his own? Why would he make something like that up? That's low, even for him. I know he's been doing the dirty on Candice with Karen but I did actually quite like the bloke, but this is way out of order. I really hope he gets his comeuppance.'

Sally put down her fork as she had now completely lost her appetite.

'It's funny you should say that' said Sally. 'I wasn't actually going to tell you as I knew you quite liked him and would have thought I was just out to get him because Karen's my friend, but seeing as you think he's a twat now as well, I'll update you.

'Go on' said Mike his attention completely focused on Sally now.

'Well, Karen sent me a text yesterday to say that she was going out to Rhodes for a few days with a couple of girls from work. She'll still be there when we dock and will be meeting us off the ship so we can have some lunch with her. I was with Anton when I got her message and we're going to arrange to walk off the ship with Simon and Candice in tow. Sort of light the touch paper, sit back and watch the fireworks!'

'I like your style' grinned Mike. 'Ordinarily I would have said that it wasn't a very nice thing to do. But in all fairness I think the bloke deserves everything that's coming to him. I just feel sorry for Karen and Candice who are really caught in the middle of it all'

'I know, but they both deserve to know what an arsehole he is. I've messaged Karen to tell her what time we will be disembarking at Rhodes. I also said that I've got something really important to tell her. Something that's best done face to face and to prepare herself for a bit of a shock'

'Oh my God' said Mike. 'She most probably thinks you're pregnant now'

'Bugger, I didn't think of that' laughed Sally. 'Mind you the amount I've been eating on this cruise I'll most probably look about 4 months gone when she sees me! But all jokes aside, we must carry on as normal and not let the creep think that anything's up otherwise it will spoil his surprise. We also need to make sure that they are with us when we get off at Rhodes, so I'll leave that one to you!'

'Yeah, thanks for that Sal. I'll try not to mess it up!'

They both had a couple of coffees and let their lunch go down, then made their way to the Spa Deck where Sally had booked them both a relaxing massage. After the conversation they had just had, a massage was the perfect tonic.

A couple of hours later they emerged from the Spa looking and feeling completely relaxed. So much so that they went straight back to their cabin, laid on the bed and fell asleep for a couple of hours. They woke up feeling refreshed and energised and decided to have dinner on their own that evening as they didn't want to spoil their chilled out mood by bumping into Simon. After a leisurely shower,

Sally phoned through to The Blue Room, one of the ships a la carte restaurants, to see if they had any tables for that evening. She knew that they wouldn't bump into Simon and Candice there as he made it quite clear the other night that he wouldn't be paying out any extra money to eat in a poncy restaurant just because it had a celebrity chef's name attached to it. Sally and Mike on the other hand couldn't wait to try it and thought the £25 per person surcharge was well worth the money. Luckily they had a table for 2 available for 7.45 so they started getting ready then had a quick G & T on the balcony before they made their way to the restaurant.

The restaurant was on the top deck and was beautifully decorated in shades of blue, hence the name Blue Room. With low lighting and soft piano music, it was a very chic and calming restaurant. They chose the 7 course tasting menu and it was outstanding. As each course was served, the waiter took time to explain exactly what they would be eating and where it was sourced from. They were also served a glass of specially selected wine that went with each plate of food. All in all it was an amazing experience and they were both glad that they had eaten there.

'Well, that was absolutely fabulous' said Mike, patting his stomach 'and all the better for not having to share it with bloody Simon!'

'Yeah, too right' agreed Sally, 'but we will have to start getting pally with him again after tonight if we want him and Candice to arrange to come off the ship with us at Rhodes. We've only got until Saturday and its Thursday tomorrow, so we haven't got that long.'

'Blimey, Thursday tomorrow, how quick is this holiday going? It only seems like yesterday that we were getting excited about boarding. Why is it that holidays always go so flaming quickly? Shame it doesn't go that quick when you're at work!'

'No, it never does' laughed Sally. 'Right I don't know about you but I'm knackered. I think we should get a bit of an early night seeing as we've got a full day out and about tomorrow. I'm really looking forward to seeing Mykonos, it's supposed to be a really lovely island.'

'Yeah I think it is' said Mike getting up from the table after leaving a large tip for the attentive staff. 'And we have definitely got a full day ahead tomorrow so you'd better get your walking shoes out! I must admit though, the island I'm really looking forward to is Santorini. But I'm sure they all have their own plusses and I am really looking forward to getting out and about for the day'

Sally and Mike made their way back to the cabin and went straight to bed, ready for an early breakfast on the balcony to watch Mykonos coming into view.

Chapter 11

At 6.30 it was already hot, even though the sun was not fully risen. The coast of Mykonos could be seen in the distance, getting nearer and nearer and the only sound that could be heard on the balcony was the gentle lapping of the crystal clear Aegean Sea. Sally and Mike's breakfast was delivered, by the ever attentive Wilson around 7 o'clock, by which time they were both showered, dressed and sitting on the balcony.

As the port got nearer, they could see the town of Mykonos (or Chora as most Greek towns with the same name as their Island are more commonly known) rise above them in a natural amphitheatre style, set around a half moon bay. The sun rising on the cube shaped houses and whitewashed walls gave it an ethereal quality as if it were an ancient land that had just been discovered.

Or as Mike put it, 'Bet they're a bugger to paint!'

'Yes, I'm sure they are Mike' said Sally, amazed that he could come out with something like that. 'But they do look beautiful, don't you think?'

'I suppose they do, yes. Just me being cynical as usual!'

'Mm' agreed Sally. 'So where are we actually going on this trip that you've booked us? I can't believe I actually let you loose on this, it better be somewhere nice'

'Oh ye of little faith' laughed Mike. 'Who's being cynical now? Right first of all we're going to the Island of Delos, which is a 40 minute ferry ride from Mykonos Town. It's the island where, in Greek mythology Zeus's mistress Leto gave birth to Apollo and Artemis and is chock a block full of ruins.'

'Wow, can't wait for that then' said Sally sarcastically. 'No wonder you told me to get my walking shoes out!'

'I know you might find it a bit boring but I love that sort of thing and it's only for a couple of hours. When we get back to Mykonos we'll have some lunch and then explore the town. It's supposed to have some fabulous shops, bars and restaurants so hopefully that will keep you happy!'

'No, I'm sure it will be a great day. You've done well and I might even let you book something else if this pans out OK!'

'Oh you're all heart, you are!' laughed Mike. 'Now finish that croissant and get your bag or we'll miss the shuttle bus to Mykonos Town where we pick up the ferry.'

They got their stuff together and disembarked with the hordes, waiting, like them, to pick up shuttle busses into town. Less than half an hour later they were sitting on the top deck of a ferry that had definitely seen better days, chugging towards Delos. The island, which was around 40 minutes away, was protected by UNESCO and was part of the world's cultural heritage. Mike was really looking forward to seeing all the ruins, Sally was just biding her time to get to the shops.

By the time the ferry docked at Delos, it was a scorching 37c and even Mike was beginning to think that perhaps this wasn't such a good idea. Luckily they had heeded advice given by the excursion team on board the ship and had slathered on high factor sun cream before leaving. They had also brought with them hats and plenty of water, which were a godsend after an hour or so of traipsing over uneven terrain where there was little or no shelter. When the tour guide escorting them around the island finally shouted out that everyone needed to start making their way back to the ferry, Sally could have kissed him.

The journey back was spent, not on the top deck like on the outbound journey, but inside in the shade, as they were both frazzled and had just about had enough sun for one day. As soon as they docked, they headed for the nearest restaurant in Mikonos Town and ordered 2 large lemonades with loads of ice. After downing those and ordering more, they were beginning to feel a little bit more human. Mike called the waiter over and asked for a couple of menus, as they were now starting to feel quite hungry.

'Bloody hell Sal, have you seen the prices in here? I hope you're not too hungry!'

'I know, they are a bit pricey but if you think I'm going to start walking round town in this heat just to save a euro or two then you can forget it. I think even if they doubled the prices I'd pay. I'm so bloody knackered I just want to sit here for an hour or so and cool off. Just order what you want, my treat!'

'Well if you put it like that' said Mike delving back into the menu. 'Perhaps it wasn't one of my better ideas to go to Delos in temperatures that high. Even I found it blooming hard going and, to be fair, it was just a load of old ruins!'

'No, not somewhere I'd rush back to, but at least we can say we've been there and not just laid on a beach! Now what are you having, I was thinking Moussaka and a large Greek salad to share?'

They didn't wait long for their lunch and when it arrived they tucked into it hungrily. Even though the prices were a bit steep, they both thought it was well worth it as the food was delicious. They ordered some coffees and then sat there for a while people watching while their lunch went down.

'Blimey Sal, it's nearly 3.30pm' said Mike looking at his watch. 'If you want to have a look round the shops we'd better get our skates on. We have to be back on the ship by 5 o'clock.'

They quickly paid the bill and wandered around the narrow, cobbled streets that were ablaze with bougainvillea, buying the odd souvenir, or in Sally's case 2 pairs of sandals, and marvelling at the beautiful windmills that graced the coastline. After about an hour, they started to make their way back to the edge of town to pick up the shuttle bus. They were just crossing over to where the bus would stop, when they heard a familiar voice behind them.

'So what did you think of Mykonos then? Bit bloody expensive wasn't it? We went back to the ship to have lunch as I certainly wasn't paying the prices here.'

Mike and Sally turned round to see Simon striding towards them with Candice tottering alongside him in 4 inch heels, barely able to stand upright on the cobbles.

'Oh we've just had a wonderful lunch in town. To be honest I didn't even look at the prices, we're on holiday so if we want it, we just have it, blow the expense!'

Sally looked at Mike in amazement and replied sarcastically. 'No, he never worries about what things costs, do you Mike?'

'Well you certainly won't keep a healthy bank balance with an outlook like that. Will they my darling?'

'No Simon they won't' said Candice, who looked like she didn't give a toss about the bank balance and just wanted to sit down somewhere.

'Oh I don't know, money isn't everything' said Mike. 'Spending time with family and friends is far more important in my view'

'Absolutely' agreed Simon. 'I didn't mean that money was more important than that, I just meant that it's nice to have a bit of money to fall back on. Anyway here comes our bus!'

Sally could see Simon was getting a bit flustered and was pleased that Mike had managed to ruffle his feathers. She was so looking forward to him getting his comeuppance on Saturday.

They got the shuttle bus back to the ship in plenty of time and agreed to meet up later in the Artemis Bar for a cocktail or two and then go to dinner in the main dining room. Mike said he'd give the others a quick ring to see if they were joining them and then book a table for around 8.30. Simon asked them if they fancied joining him for some tea and cake from the buffet but, after the day that they'd had, Sally and Mike declined and made their way back to their cabin for a shower and a lie down. After phoning the others, who were all up for joining them, and making arrangements to meet in the bar, they both showered and had an hours sleep, waking up feeling much better than they did earlier.

Sally and Mike were the first to arrive at the bar and ordered the cocktail of the day, which was a delicious frozen mango Daiquiri. In fact they were halfway through their second one before the first of their dinner companions, Anton, turned up.

'Blimey, you two are hitting the hard stuff tonight, aren't you' he laughed as he sat himself down on a bar stool, next to Sally. He ordered another couple of Daiquiris for them and a Pink Porn Star for himself.

'Really, a Pink Porn Star!' laughed Sally. 'Only you could order a cocktail with a name like that! Perhaps you could order one for Simon when he turns up'

'I would darling, but unfortunately they don't have one called a Cheating Twat'

'Who's a cheating twat?' said a voice behind them.

'Oh, Simon, Candice. Sorry didn't see you there' said Sally desperately trying to think of a way to explain Anton's remark.

'Oh, we were just talking about an old ex of mine' interjected Anton in the nick of time. 'I was telling Sally and Mike how I came home one night and caught him with a woman. The humiliation was excruciating, I can tell you. Anyway can I offer you both a Pink Porn Star?'

'No, it's OK, I think I'll stick to a man's drink if it's all the same to you' said Simon, looking at Anton as if he was off another planet. 'But, I'm sure Candy will have one though. She likes anything that's pink and girly!'

Anton would have loved to have knocked that smug look right off his face but he managed to rein his anger in and ordered him a pint of lager, desperately wishing he could lace it with something nasty.

While they were waiting for the others to arrive, Mike turned the conversation to the next couple of ports they were visiting and asked Simon what his plans were.

'Well I don't think we'll be going anywhere tomorrow when we dock at Kos. I've heard some horrible things about all those bloody refugees that seem to have taken over the island. I don't think either myself or Candy really want to be accosted by any of them so we'll stay on the ship where we'll be safe. Surely you won't be venturing off will you?'

'God I can't believe what comes out of that man's mouth' whispered Anton to Sally. 'Not only is he homophobic, he's now a bloody racist. Does he have any redeeming qualities?'

'OK' whispered Sally 'let me think about that one. No he doesn't!'

'You can't believe everything you read in the papers, Simon' said Mike in answer to his question and astounded by his prejudiced outburst, 'So, yes we're definitely going to be having a look around Kos Town. In fact we'll most probably stay and have some lunch there. You're more than welcome to join us. But if you don't fancy Kos, what about Rhodes? I've heard Rhodes Town is absolutely stunning. Full of history, with some fabulous shops for the ladies. Again, you're more that welcome to tag along, we'll be leaving the ship around 10am on Saturday if you're up for it!'

'Oh let's go with them Simon. I really fancy seeing Rhodes' cried Candice, pleading with him.

'Yeah, why not. It will be good fun' said Simon to Mike. 'It's a date. Will you be coming along Anton?'

'Oh, I may just come along for the ride. It's not like I've got a full diary or anything!'

'Good, that's that settled then. Rhodes on Saturday it is' said Mike, pleased with himself for managing to arrange to get Simon off the ship and into the clutches of Karen. 'Oh look, here come the others.'

When everyone had a drink in their hand and a seat at the bar, Mike asked around to see if anyone else wanted to go ashore to Kos with him and Sally the next day. Anton said he was going with Hannah and Richard on the day trip to Bodrum in Turkey.

'You're more than welcome to join us if you want. I'm sure there are tickets still available' both Hannah and Richard nodded in agreement with Anton.

'Thanks for asking Hun' said Sally, 'but the one and only time that we went to Turkey, Mike was really ill. We had to get the doctor in and everything. It was a few years ago but he still goes white if you mention it!'

'Yeah, I think I'll stick to Greece if it's all the same with you. But I'm sure you'll all have a fabulous time' joked Mike sticking his fingers in his mouth to mimic throwing up.

'What about you Valerie? I hope you're not going to stay on the ship on your own. You know you're more than welcome to come ashore with us' said Sally

'No, you're alright love. I've agreed to meet those ladies again. You know the ones I met up with in Casino. We're going to have a wander round castle then have some lunch or maybe even go to the beach for a swim'

'OK' said Sally. 'As long as you're sure? I'd hate the thought of you being left on board on your own for the day. Now who's up for getting some food? I don't know about you lot but my stomach is growling!'

The rest of the evening passed without incident and even Simon and Anton managed to hold a conversation, albeit a very small one, without sniping at each other. The food was, as usual, outstanding and they all went to bed that night completely full and contented.

Chapter 12

The next morning dawned as radiant as the previous and, once again, Sally and Mike had their breakfast on the balcony while watching the ship sail into Kos Town.
'So, what do you think of this cruising lark then?' asked Mike. 'Is it what you imagined or better?'
'Oh loads better. I'd definitely do it again, wouldn't you?'
'Oh yes, without a doubt. I'd do it again just for the food, it's been amazing' agreed Mike, tucking into his fourth pastry. 'But, food aside, we've seen some fabulous places and met some really lovely people. Apart from Simon that is, but I bet we'll even be talking about him for years to come!'
'Especially after tomorrow' laughed Sally. 'She's a funny one though, that Hannah, don't you think? Richard is a really lovely bloke, really friendly and outgoing but she's so hard work. She always looks like she's about to burst into tears, and I think she may have an eating disorder'.
'What makes you think that then? Can't say I've taken an awful lot of notice of her. As you say, she's bloody hard work'
'Well, she doesn't eat a lot and she's always pushing her food around on the plate, then making a big show of feeling full up. And Richard quite often tells us that she's either feeling sick or being sick. I reckon she's bulimic or something. She's not right, that's for sure'
'No, I suppose she's not but it's not really our business and Richard has never hinted that anything is wrong, so perhaps it's best we just let them get on with it'
'Yeah, you're right I suppose' agreed Sally. 'Now where's that camera, we're almost in port and we haven't taken any pictures yet this morning'.
It seemed as if everyone on the ship were standing on their balconies watching the Grecian Princess, once again, effortlessly slip

into her berth and the sound of cameras clicking was almost deafening.

'I can't believe Simon and Candice aren't getting off the ship here. It looks absolutely beautiful' said Sally putting the last of her stuff in her bag.

'No, neither can I. That man has got such petty prejudices. Still his loss. Right, are we ready? At least we haven't got to bother with shuttle buses today, we can just stroll out into town'

The harbour of Kos Town was dominated by the impressive Neratzia Castle which was built by the Knights Templar. In front of the castle walls was the town centre beach with a second, bigger beach, just north of the harbour. With the main town full of shops, bars and restaurants, as well as a plethora of ruins and architecture, this really was a place that looked as though it would cater for everyone.

Sally and Mike, along with hordes of sightseers from, not only their ship, but the even bigger American ship that had docked alongside theirs, made their way into the town. Kos Town looked as if it was going to be very busy.

After having a stroll around some of the many shops, they found a fabulous little indoor market on Eleftherias Street. It wasn't massive but it was full of little gifts such as handmade olive oil soaps, honey and glyko tomataki (candied tomato sweets) – which were actually more tasty than they sounded. It was also where the locals came to buy their fruit and veg and the smell of all the fresh herbs was intoxicating. Once they had exhausted all it had to offer, they made their way back towards the castle and found a pavement café to sit for a while and people watch whilst having a couple of glasses of Mythos.

It was while they were on their second cold beer that Mike noticed Valerie walking along the street towards where they were sitting.

'Sal, didn't you say that Valerie was going to the castle with a couple of ladies that she'd met in the Casino?'

'Yeah, she's been going off with them most evenings I think. It's nice that she's made some friends on ship'

'I'm sure it is but she's definitely not with a couple of ladies now, in fact she's arm in arm with a bloke.'

'Where? You must be seeing things. Oh my God, you're right. And they're heading this way. We'd better pretend we haven't seen them' said Sally opening up her phone to look at it.

'You've got to be joking' said Mike as he called out to her. 'I want to know who this bloke is!'

As Mike called her name, Valerie looked over and saw him and Sally. She looked rather sheepish but came over to their table all the same.

'Hello you two, who'd have thought you'd have seen me out of all these people here'

'I know' smiled Mike, looking over at the man Valerie was arm in arm with. 'It's a small world isn't it?'

'Yes, it certainly is! Sorry, where's my manners. This is Fergus. Fergus, this is Sally and Mike from the ship. Do you remember I told you about how we met on the first night on a shared table and then found out that I knew Sally from going to the same slimming club in Norfolk'

Fergus shook hands with Mike and gave Sally a peck on the cheek.

'Yes, I remember you saying. It's lovely to meet you both, Valerie's told me a lot about you, all good by the way! I hope you're having a great time on board'

'Oh, we're having a lovely time thanks Fergus' said Sally 'It's our first cruise but it certainly won't be our last, that's for sure. What about you, have you cruised before?'

'Yes, you could say that' said Fergus grinning.

'So Valerie, I thought you were going out with the two ladies you made friends with.'

'Ah' said Valerie, looking rather guilty. 'There are no ladies, I've actually been meeting up with Fergus all this time. We met on the first day of the cruise and got on really well so we've had a couple of dates on and off the ship. We're both newly single and both seem to like the same things, so why not!'

'Why on earth didn't you tell us that then?' asked Sally. 'It's not like you're doing anything you shouldn't, is it?'

'No, not really, but the problem is' explained Fergus 'that I work with the Shore Excursion Team on board the ship and we're not supposed to fraternise with the guests, so that's the reason why we've had to keep it under wraps. Once we dock back in Corfu, I'm on leave for a couple of weeks and we are going to stay on the island for little holiday, so we can see where it goes from there but until then, can we ask you not to tell anyone about us?'

'Oh of course you can, our lips are sealed' exclaimed Sally. 'I think it's really sweet that you met on board, how romantic!'

'Thanks Sally, suppose it is really, but I'm a bit old in the tooth for all this undercover lark. Still I never had this sort of excitement when I were with Brian, so I'm not complaining! Right then, we're off to the castle now so I'll see you most probably at the bar before dinner'

Sally and Mike said their goodbyes to Valerie and Fergus and finished their beers.

'Well who'd have thought it? It's one scandal after another on this holiday' laughed Mike as he called the waiter over to pay their bill. 'Right, I don't know about you but I fancy a swim before we have some lunch'.

They both headed towards the harbour and the small beach that was in front of the castle. It wasn't the best beach in the world, quite small and pebbled, but it would do for the purpose of just having a swim. Luckily they had the forethought of putting their swimming things on under their clothes and packing a couple of beach towels, along with the rest of the stuff that Sally felt she needed to pack for a couple of hours off the ship! After having a welcoming swim in the warm waters of the Mediterranean, they dried off and went to get some lunch in one of the many harbour-side restaurants.

They found a lovely, traditional taverna, literally a stones' throw from the harbour wall and sat for an hour or so people watching and taking in the beauty of the sites, whilst sampling the local Symi Shrimps that everyone had been raving about. These tiny, pink prawns that were fried and coated in a tomato sauce, were so delicate that they could be eaten whole with the shells on. The only things needed to accompany them were some freshly baked bread and a carafe of wine. Sally and Mike both thought that it was the best seafood dish they had ever tasted.

'I still can't believe Valerie, sneaking off to meet Fergus' said Mike, mopping up the last of his sauce with a massive chunk of bread.

'It is a bit cloak and dagger isn't it' agreed Sally. 'But, to be fair, you wouldn't want to see the man lose his job and some of these companies are really funny about staff having relationships with guests'.

'Mm, I suppose you're right. Does seem a bit petty if you ask me though. They're both single and both over the age of consent, so I don't see what the harm is. But hey, ho, who am I to argue with the laws of a mighty shipping company! Now shall we order some coffees and perhaps a small portion of baklava to share?'

'Share! Baklava!' gasped Sally, horrified. 'I'm not sharing mine with anyone. Get your own!'

They finished their coffees and the, not so small, portions of baklava and started to walk back to the ship

'So tomorrow's the day old Simon gets his comeuppance then' said Mike as they stood waiting to get back on board the ship.

'I know, it's weird really. I've waited all this time for him to get what's coming to him and now that it's about to happen, I'm wondering whether I'm doing the right thing or not!'

Mike turned to face Sally. 'Don't start having second thoughts now babe. The man deserves everything he gets. It's not your fault that Karen decided to spring a visit on us, and it's better she finds out what he's like now, after only a few months instead of leaving it and her getting hurt in a couple of years' time. All we're doing is walking off the ship with him, we'll let Karen take over from there. And anyway, you can't back out now, this is the highlight of Anton's holiday!'

'I suppose you're right' agreed Sally. 'He is a complete bastard and, as you say, all I'm doing is walking off the ship with him. But, saying that, I still can't wait until tomorrow is over'.

By the time they got on board and back to their cabin, it was getting on for 4 o'clock, so they decided just to sit on the balcony and read for an hour or so. After they had watched the ship slowly push off from its' berth and slip out to sea they started getting ready to go to dinner.

They all met in the Artemis Bar for drinks at 7.30 and Sally still couldn't help thinking that perhaps she was doing the wrong thing by meeting Karen, with Simon and Candice in tow. But after listening to a conversation that Mike was having with Anton about Lucy, Sally knew she was definitely doing the right thing.

Mike had been telling Anton all about his daughter Lucy who lives in Cyprus and how he tries to get out there as much as possible to see her, when Simon piped up.

'Wow, didn't know your daughter lived in Cyprus mate. That's a bit of a way to go and see her isn't it?'

'Yes I suppose it is' agree Mike 'but, at the end of the day, she is my daughter and, to be fair, even if she moved to Mars we'd still find a way to go and visit her.'

'Bloody right we would' interjected Sally, who could see where this conversation was heading. 'Lucy's not even my daughter but she's part of Mike's life so that makes her part of mine too. Now I'm not at work, we'll be able to get out there a lot more, which I'm really looking forward to as we get on like a house on fire'

'Oh absolutely' said Simon. 'It's great that you get on well with her, Sally. Some women would not want to take on someone else's child – even though she's hardly a child. But you know what I mean. In fact I really don't think people should have kids if they're not prepared to take the good times with the bad or put themselves out occasionally. I know if I had been fortunate enough to have children, we would have followed them to the ends of the earth, wouldn't we darling?'

Candice nodded in agreement. 'Oh yes, even if Simon had children from a previous relationship, I would have welcomed them with open arms. But I'm afraid we'll never have that opportunity. But hey, these things happen and at least we've got each other.'

Sally and Mike were gobsmacked. They stood and looked at Simon in amazement. Astounded at how easy the lies tripped off his tongue. Sally actually felt sorry for Candice and hoped she dumped the rat and found someone who could treat her with respect. She was actually now looking forward to tomorrow, a lot!

Chapter 13

Sally went to bed that night thinking she would be laying there for hours, turning things over in her head. But as it happened, she fell asleep almost as soon as her head hit the pillow. She awoke just before Mike, feeling refreshed and ready for the day ahead.

They got showered and dressed, after having a cuppa on the balcony to watch the port of Rhodes come into view, then made their way up to the restaurant where they were meeting Anton, Simon and Candice. As they weren't meeting Karen until about 10 o'clock they decided they would have a leisurely breakfast, or the last supper as Anton eloquently put it, before making their way off the ship.

Simon and Candice were already seated on a table for 6, by the window, and waved them over. Anton wasn't far behind them and once they had all sat down the waiter came over to take their order.

The boys all had the full English and Candice had scrambled egg on toast, but although Sally's stomach was growling, she really couldn't face eating a big breakfast so just ordered some toast and jam.

'Are sure that's all you want Sal?' asked Mike, 'you normally load right up on the breakfasts'

'No, I'm fine babe. I'm just not that hungry this morning. I'll most probably make up for it lunchtime though!'

As they sat eating their breakfasts, Simon became quite animated, looking straight past Sally out of the window behind her.

'Do you two know anyone in Rhodes?' he asked Mike and Sally

'No, I don't think so' answered Mike, 'Why do you ask?'

'Well, there's some woman on the dockside holding up a placard saying "Good Morning Sally and Mike" so I assumed it was someone you know'

Sally quickly turned round to look out of the window and there was Karen, bold as brass holding her placard and waving like mad.

'Oh my God, it's Karen' she said to Mike.

'Whose Karen then?' asked Simon 'One of your friends, I take it? Obviously you wasn't expecting this, by the look on your face! I think it's quite funny actually and nice of her to come and meet you both at the ship.'

'You don't know who she is then?' asked Sally, a feeling of dread washing over her.

'Me' exclaimed Simon. 'No, never seen her before in my life, why should I have?'

'Sal?' questioned Mike looking really worried.

'Shit' said Sally burying her head in her hands. 'Mike, can I have a quick word with you back at the cabin. We'll meet you all back here in 20 minutes, OK? Just something I need to sort out'

Mike walked out after Sally who was racing ahead and caught up with her at the lift.

'Sal, hold on love I'm out of breath. What the bloody hell was that all about?'

'He doesn't even know her, does he? Not an ounce of recognition. I think I've got the wrong bloke. How could I be so bloody stupid? I was so sure it was him. I've made myself look a right pratt now haven't I?'

'Well, it's not too bad, it was only me and Anton that you told. At least Simon doesn't know anything or any of the others for that fact. Look, let's go back, get the rest of them and meet Karen and then we can all have a bloody good laugh about it!'

'I'm not sure anyone's going to find it that funny to be honest. I've slagged the poor bloke off all week, looked forward to his wife dumping him and it wasn't even the right person. I feel terrible. It did look like him though and I'm sure Karen said he is an estate agent in Kent. Although knowing my bloody memory lately, he could have just as easily been a travel agent in Ghent!'

'I really wouldn't worry Sal, there's been no harm done and I'm sure everyone will see the funny side of it when you tell them. Right we'd better go back and explain to Anton that you got your wires crossed. Actually, we don't need to, here he comes'.

'Sally, are you alright my dear. You looked like you had seen a ghost earlier. Whatever is the matter?'

'Oh Anton' cried Sally. 'I've made a right pratt of myself. Did you see Simon's face when he saw Karen? He didn't have a clue who she was. It looks like he's not the bloke that she's been seeing after all. I can't believe I condemned the man without getting my facts right'

'Don't worry about it Sally' laughed Anton. 'I do it all the time, I'm terrible with faces and to be fair, he might not be guilty of sleeping with your friend but he is still a bit of a knob! Anyway, it's not like you accused him outright is it? The only people that know are us three standing here so there's no real harm done'.

'No I suppose your right Anton' agreed Sally, feeling better already. 'It could have been a lot worse. But I am going to tell them once we meet up with Karen and hopefully they'll both understand. Right, I suppose we'd better go and get Simon and Candice and face the music!'

The three of them made their way back the restaurant where Simon and Candice were waiting outside for them, looking quite concerned.

'Are you OK Sally, you looked quite peaky there earlier? Are you sure you still want to go ashore today?'

'Absolutely' said Sally, giving them both a hug. 'I just want to say sorry'

'Sorry for what' said Simon, looking extremely baffled.

'I'll tell you when we get off here and meet up with Karen'

'Now I'm even more confused. Who is this Karen? I take it she's the same one that was standing on the quayside with the placard?'

'Yeah, she's a very good friend of mine and is out here for a few days holiday and decided to come and meet us off the ship so we could have some lunch together'.

'Oh right, it all makes sense now!' said Simon 'But, surely if you're meeting up with your friend you won't want us two tagging along with you. We'll go off on our own and meet up with you later.'

'No please, you both need to come along' insisted Sally. 'There's something I need to explain to you and I just hope you see the funny side of it!'

'OK, if you're sure?' said Simon, looking very confused.

They had all brought their bags with them to breakfast, so no-one needed to go back to their cabin and they could go straight down to the deck where everyone was disembarking. As soon as they stepped off the gangplank, Sally could see Karen waving frantically at them from behind the barriers at the port. She ran the short way over to her and gave her a big hug.

'Oh my God, am I glad to see you'

'Really Sal, didn't think you'd miss me this much' laughed Karen, prising Sally off her. 'I thought you were having a really good time?'

'Oh we are Karen, it's been amazing. I think I can honestly say it's one of the best holidays we've been on. There was just a little blip due to me getting my wires crossed, as usual. I'll tell you all about it later when we find somewhere to have a drink. Come on I'll introduce you to some of the people we've met on the ship. You don't mind them coming into town with us do you?'

'No of course I don't, the more the merrier. Hello Mike, how are you?'

Mike gave Karen a big hug and introduced her to Simon, Candice and Anton and then they all made their way out of the port and towards Rhodes old town, which Mike had previously enthused about.

Chapter 14

They decided to start off by having a walk around the medieval walled city which is, as Mike informed them, the biggest and most preserved medieval settlement in Europe. This fabulous city full of inns that were used by the Knights, Gothic churches, palaces and mosques was fascinating, even to Sally and Karen, who would normally head for the more modern part of town where the shops were! Walking along the narrow stone-paved alleyways, past traditional Rhodean houses and mansions, they occasional came across palm trees and exquisite fountains, which added to the beauty of this living history book. It truly was a magical place to see and they were all extremely glad that they had taken Mike's lead and visited it.

As the city was surrounded by huge stone walls, it soon became unbearably hot and they started to look around for somewhere in the shade to get some refreshment. Simon was the first to spot such a place, a little restaurant tucked away in a courtyard that afforded them the shade they desperately needed. They all sat down and ordered some drinks and some little cheese and spinach pies to munch on while they chatted.

'So, what's this little "blip" you were talking about then Sal?' asked Karen.

'Yes, I'm very intrigued as well' added Simon. 'What was it exactly that you were sorry for earlier?'

'Well, it's a bit embarrassing to tell the truth' admitted Sally, looking very sheepish.

'Oh go on Sal, when have you ever been embarrassed?' laughed Karen.

'OK. It's about Simon, the bloke you've been seeing. Well I could have sworn you said he was an Estate Agent in Kent and he does look at bit Spanish. So when I met Simon and Candice here, I stupidly assumed the worst!'

'Please tell me you didn't think that me and him' said Karen pointing to Simon, 'were have an away day? Sorry, no offence mate'

'None taken Karen. Sally did you really think that I was seeing your friend behind Candy's back?' asked Simon looking quite affronted. 'I would never cheat on her. I can't believe you didn't say something to me, at least I could have put you straight.'

'I know, I should have but I was absolutely convinced that you were Karen's Simon and the more I thought about it, the more I disliked you. When you said that you got married in June in Spain, I remembered that Karen had said that her Simon had been to a funeral in Spain around that time and I thought that's just what you told her and you were really getting married! It really took a turn for the worst when you were talking about not being able to have children and I remember Karen saying to me that her Simon had grown up children from a previous marriage that he never bothered seeing. I thought you was a right bastard. The plan was to walk off the ship with you so that Karen could see what a two-timing rat she had been seeing. I realised I had the wrong person when we saw Karen from the ship and you had no idea who she was. Now you know why I am apologising.'

'Blimey, no wonder you didn't like him!' said Karen 'Actually sitting here listening to you talking about him has only strengthened my resolve to dump him Sal. I've been thinking of doing it for a while now and actually came away to think it through. He's been nothing but agro since we met and, to be honest, I really don't know what I saw in him. But, going back to what you originally said, my Simon, or should I say my ex, is from Kent but he's not an Estate Agent, he's a builder. He is half Spanish though, I think on his Mum's side and he did go to a funeral in Spain but it was in April and only for a couple of days. I don't suppose you're Spanish are you Simon?'

'No, not even slightly, Kent born and bred. My Mum and Dad do live out there though. They retired to the Costa Blanca a couple of years ago, so that probably where the Spanish connection comes from'

'Oh God, I made a right balls up didn't I?'

'Yep, I'm afraid you did Sal' laughed Karen. 'Though to be fair, when I first told you about Simon, it was just after your Mum had passed away and you really wasn't yourself, so I'm not surprised you didn't take it all in, and you have done me a massive favour in making my mind up about him, so don't feel too bad about it. Hang on a minute, I think I might have a picture of him in my bag somewhere.'

After a rummage around in her handbag, Karen pulled out a photo and showed it to everyone. It looked nothing like Simon, as was expected.

'Oh no!' exclaimed Sally holding the photo up next to Simon. 'Even the photo doesn't look like you. What a pratt. I can't believe I thought that it did.'

'Sally, please don't worry about it. There's been no harm done and I really haven't taken offence to it. In fact it's given everyone a good old laugh, and made Karen's mind up to dump him, so let's just forget it. But I will let you buy me a cocktail or two when we get back on board just to show no hard feelings!'

'Oh I do hope they'll be Pink Porn Stars' laughed Anton.

'Sorry to disappoint you Anton but the answer's still no. Actually, thinking about it I might just stick to a couple of pints of lager if it's all the same with you, Sally. But if you really want to Anton, you can dress them up with umbrellas and sparklers!'

'You're on' said Anton, slowly starting to warm to Simon.

They ordered some more drinks and chatted to Karen about events on the ship, causing her to nearly choke on her beer when Anton described how they found Prudence and George. After a few more similar stories, the earlier events concerning Sally's mistaken identity were all but forgotten and everyone was getting on like a house on fire.

'So, we know you're an Estate Agent Simon, but what about you Candice, do you work?' asked Karen, eager to find out more about her new friends.

'Yeah, I work in the retail industry' replied Candice.

'Oh right. What shop do you work in?'

'Well, it's sort of an animal feed outlet'

'I really can't image you working in a pet shop' said Mike, 'I had you down as more of a boutique kind of girl!'

'Actually, my wife is far too modest. She doesn't work in a pet shop, she owns a chain of animal food outlets that distribute to pet shops, stables and vets all over the country. A very astute business woman is Candy'

No-one could believe what Simon had just told them and it must have shown on their faces, especially Sally, who looked completely gobsmacked.

'I always get that reaction when people find out what I do for a living' laughed Candice. 'Most people think I work in a boutique or a beauticians or something. In fact I only dress like this when I'm on holiday or at a party. You wouldn't recognise me at home with no make-up, hair tied back and jeans and wellies on!'

'Well, it just goes to show you should never judge a book by its cover' laughed Karen.

'Tell me about it' whispered Sally to Anton 'I thought she worked on the tills in a supermarket. Who'd have thought?'

Once they had finished their drinks, they carried on walking round the old town until they came out besides the port again. A little further along, they eventually came to the new part of town which was a mass of modern shops, bars, restaurants and plush hotels. The girls were in seventh heaven and made a few dents in their credit cards by buying shoes, bags and perfume for themselves, along with some gifts for people back home.

After doing some serious shopping, Karen suggested they stop for lunch at a quaint looking Italian Pizzeria that was hidden away in a back street. She told them that she had heard about the place from friends who had eaten there many times over the years and who promised her that it served the best pizza outside Italy. No-body needed persuading and they followed Karen into the restaurant.

The inside of the Pizzeria looked really authentic and was decked out in red and white checked tablecloths, complete with wine bottle candle holders on each table. Pictures of Italy graced the walls and the waiters looked like they had just stepped out from a Dolmio advert! Large overhead fans kept the place nice and cool, which was what they needed after traipsing around the shops in 40c heat.

They all ordered pizzas, plates of bruschetta, and a glass each of the house red, which was extremely good. Just as Karen had promised, these were the best pizzas any of them had ever tasted and no-one left as much as a crust. Just as they were finishing up eating, the waiter came over with a couple of bottles of Prosecco and a large chocolate birthday cake, resplendent with sparklers and candles.

'I do think that perhaps they might have the wrong table' whispered Anton. 'Awkward. That is unless it is somebody's birthday?'

'Oh God no, Karen you haven't?' groaned Sally.

'Oh yes I have' she admitted 'This lunch is on me today. Let's just call it a little pre-Birthday treat as I won't see you on the actual day, and by the look on everyone's faces Sal, I take it you haven't told them that it's your 50th Birthday on Wednesday!'

'No, I was hoping to keep it quiet actually. It's not something I'm really looking forward to'

'Fat chance of that my dear, now everyone knows your little secret' grinned Anton. 'Wednesday you say, Karen? Well, I'm going to make sure that you have a 50th to remember Sally. We will all celebrate your birthday with you in true style and I'll make sure there are plenty of photos for you to see Karen'

'Thanks Anton, I'll look forward to seeing them. Now, who's up for chocolate cake and Prosecco?'

They sat eating, drinking and chatting for another hour or so before making their way back in to town. By the time they had popped into the last couple of shops that they had missed the first time round, it was getting on for 5 o'clock.

'Blimey, I've just seen the time' said Karen to Sally, looking quite worried. 'When have you lot got to be back on board?'

'It's OK Karen, we don't have to be back until 8pm tonight as it's a late sailing'

'Don't you have to be at dinner for a certain time though?'

'No, we're alright actually' answered Simon. 'We're all booked, on what they call, Freedom Dining, where you can choose what restaurant you want to eat in and at what time. But after the amount we've eaten today I might just give dinner a miss tonight and perhaps go and visit the midnight buffet this evening. I don't know what everyone else fancies doing?'

'You know what Simon, that's a bloody good idea you've just had' nodded Anton. 'I for one will certainly be joining you, it's not like we've got to get up early in the morning, seeing as we are at sea all day tomorrow. So who else is up for a late one?'

'Sounds good to me mate' agreed Mike. 'We'll just have to get hold of Richard and Hannah and Valerie when we get back on board and see if they fancy it too. I've never been to a midnight buffet before and I've heard this one involves quite a bit of chocolate. I just hope I can stay awake that long!'

'Oh, I wish I was coming back to the ship with you' said Karen wistfully. 'It sounds amazing. I suppose I'll have to make do with a couple of gyros and a bar crawl round Faliraki!'

'Like you won't enjoy that!' laughed Sally, knowing her friend liked nothing more than a good skinful, washed down with some junk food.

'Yeah, I probably will' laughed Karen, 'even if I can't remember it tomorrow! Right, I'd better be off then. I need to catch my bus back to the hotel in 20 minutes. It was really great meeting up with you and Mike and it was lovely meeting you the rest of you. I hope you all have a fabulous last week of cruising and Sal, have an amazing birthday.'

Everyone said their goodbyes to Karen, thanking her for treating them all to lunch, and then they started to make their way back to the ship.

'She's lovely, your friend Karen, isn't she?' said Simon to Sally as they walked along. 'In fact I almost wish I was "her Simon"!'

'Dream on fat boy!' said Candice, punching him in the arm.

'Only joking sweetheart, you know I've only got eyes for you! Right then, what time are we all going to meet in the bar?'

'Well, by the time we get back it'll be gone 6 o'clock and, I don't know about you' grimaced Candice, 'but my feet are killing me so I may have to have a lay down for a while and get Simon to massage them!

'Yeah, me too' agreed Sally, 'Well, obviously not the foot massage bit cause that would be a bit weird, but I do need a lay down. As we're not going to have dinner tonight, why don't we meet in the bar between 9 and 9.30? That gives us time to have showers and a bit of a nap. I'll give Valerie a call and see if she's up for it, if you two can call Richard and Hannah'

'No problem. We'll see you both in the bar later then'

Chapter 15

As soon as they got back to their cabin, Sally put away her bags of shopping and called Valerie, to make arrangements for that evening. She wasn't in her cabin so Sally left a message on her phone to tell her that they would be in the bar after 9 o'clock if she wanted to join them. She then made a couple of mugs of tea and both her and Mike kicked off their shoes and laid on the bed to watch the news and see what was happening in the world.

'That was really nice of Karen to treat us all to lunch like that, she didn't have to do it'

'Yeah, it was' agreed Mike, 'especially when she thought it would only be us two meeting her. I did offer to pay for the others but she wasn't having any of it'.

'That's Karen all over though. The only problem now, is that they all know I'm going to be 50 in a couple of days' time. I was hoping to keep that quite but I've got no chance now, have I? That's Karma for thinking terrible things about Simon. I still can't believe how wrong I got that. At least everyone saw the funny side of it'.

'Yeah, I do think you may have got away with that one' agreed Mike 'and what about Candice? Who would have thought she was a successful business woman, especially in that sort of industry?'

'No, I would never have guessed that in a million years. I'd love to see her in jeans and wellies with no make-up on!'

'I can't wait to tell the others about Simon. Richard will crease up. You never know, even Hannah might crack her dial!'

'Oh alright, let's have a fun evening at my expense. I suppose I'll be the butt of everyone's jokes for the rest of the cruise now!'

'Well you do ask for it sometimes Sal! Right, turn that telly off, I don't know about you but I'm knackered. I've put the alarm on for quarter to 8, just in case we overdo it'.

And with that, they both fell sound asleep, waking only when the alarm went off.

They crawled out of bed and managed to shower, get dressed and be in the bar by 9 o'clock, beaten only by Anton who was already at the bar, armed with one of his neon pink cocktails.

'Glad you could make it' he said sarcastically.

'What? I thought we'd be the first here. It is only 9 o'clock' said Mike.

'Yes, but we said to meet here between 8 and 8.30, didn't we?'

'Oh Anton, I'm so glad I'm not the only one losing the plot' laughed Sally. 'We arranged to meet here between 9 and 9.30. Please tell me you haven't been sitting here on your own for an hour!'

'Actually, I haven't. I've had Felix here to keep me company' said Anton pointing to the barman. 'He's been telling me all about the irrigation methods his father uses on their farm back in India. It's been so interesting' Anton stifled a yawn and rolled his eyes 'but I am rather glad that you two have finally turned up'.

'Well we can always go again if you're having fun without us' joked Sally.

'Don't you dare! Now what do you want to drink the pair of you. Oh, here come the others now, this is turning into a dear round!'

They all got their drinks and relocated to a large table by the window, not far from where a pianist was playing in the corner. To say he wasn't great on the ivories was the understatement of the year but they had great fun trying to decipher which tunes he was playing and it wasn't long before they abandoned the cocktails in favour of bottles of Prosecco, that is apart from Hannah who seemed to think that more than one glass of alcohol gave her heartburn. Sally did offer her some indigestion tablets but she declined and started drinking lemonade.

Talk inevitably got round to the events earlier in the day and Sally, Mike and Simon filled the others in as to how Sally had mistaken Simon for Karen's boyfriend. Mike was right, even Hannah had a good laugh about it, which was amazing as she was probably the only sober one amongst them.

'So what was it that really made you dislike Simon then? That's if sleeping with your best friend wasn't enough!' asked Richard.

'I think it was when poor old Simon was talking to Mike about him and Candice not being able to have children and I knew that Karen's Simon had two grown up boys from his first marriage that he never bothered seeing. That really made me angry. Obviously now I know that they really can't have children, I feel terrible'

'Oh that's OK' said Candice 'it's not your fault. We've sort of got our heads round it now. It was hard at first because I would have loved to have had a couple of kids but if that's how it is then we've just got to get over it. It can be difficult though sometimes when you see women who have kids just for the sake of it, because their mates are having them, or to get them on the council house list. And women who use abortion as a form of contraception really piss me off. They see pregnancy as some sort of inconvenience that they can just make disappear when it doesn't suit, when some women would give their right hand to fall pregnant. But what can you do?

Anyway, sorry, I'm rambling now, I think it's the Prosecco talking. Let's get back to the silliness!'

Mike started telling everyone about the picture of Karen's ex that she showed them, when Sally noticed that Hannah, who was staring out the window, was starting to look as if her whole world was about to crumble.

Sally leant over to her and discretely asked if she was alright. She obviously wasn't and when she turned towards Sally she could see tears welling up in her eyes.

'OK, let's go to the loo and sort this out then' said Sally, getting Hannah up, taking her by the arm and steering her away from the others.

'It's alright, nothing to worry about, Hannah's got a piece of mascara in her eye, we're just going to the ladies so I can help her get it out' Sally informed the rest of them before they had the chance to question Hannah's tears.

By the time they got into the ladies, Hannah was in floods of tears. Sally put her arm around her and tried to comfort her as best she could but she could feel her body being wracked by huge sobs. She let her cry it out for a while before tentatively asking what the problem was.

'I am so sorry about this' gulped Hannah between sobs.

'Whatever is the matter sweetheart?' asked Sally pulling off reams of loo roll to help mop up the tears.

'I'm pregnant' cried Hannah

'Oh, wow, that's brilliant. Isn't it?'

'No that's the problem, it's not. I'm 46 years of age and I really thought I was going through the menopause. But obviously I wasn't because now I'm nearly 3 months gone.'

'Blimey, a bit of a shock then' admitted Sally

'Yeah, you could say that' agreed Hannah, blowing her nose. 'We both decided when we first got married that we didn't really want kids and we were more than happy, just the two of us, spending our hard earned money on a nice home and 2 or 3 holidays a year. We've never regretted not having them, in fact Richard always says it's the best decision we ever made and a few weeks ago I would have agreed with him. But, in the last couple of weeks my hormones have gone into overdrive and all my maternal instincts have kicked in big time. I was all set for an abortion when I first found out I was pregnant but now I really don't think I can do it. The only problem is Richard. He is going to be so angry that this has happened and I really don't want to lose him but I also don't want to lose this baby. I haven't got a clue what to do Sal'.

'Yeah you're right, that is a bit of a dilemma but, you're not going to know what Richard thinks until you tell him are you? You can't keep it a secret for ever and you're going to have to make a decision about what to do pretty soon. Tell him tonight. What's the worst that could happen? He's hardly going to chuck you overboard. I'm sure you'll be pleasantly surprised about how understanding he is, and if he's not then he's really not worth it. Promise me you'll go and get him now and tell him'

'I don't know, I've been trying to pluck up the courage the whole time I've been on this cruise, but as you said, I can't keep up this pretence much longer, it's not fair to any of us. I really appreciate you listening to me, Sal. I can't promise, but I'm really going to try and tell him tonight. I've kept this bottled up for so long it's been making me ill.'

'I thought it had' said Sally. 'In fact I actually thought you had some sort of eating disorder as you kept picking at your food and being sick!'

'I suppose it did look like that, to be honest, and I've been so depressed about it, you all must have thought I was a right miserable cow'

'Well, now you mention it!' laughed Sally. 'Come on, let's get back to the others and you can go and tell Richard your news. If you still need a shoulder to cry on, you know where I am'

'Thanks Sal, I really appreciate you being here for me. Now I suppose I'd better get it over with'

When they got back to the bar, Hannah had a quiet word with Richard and they made their excuses and left.

'What's going on there then?' asked Mike. 'It all looks a bit serious!'

'Oh just women's problems, nothing to worry about' said Sally to everyone, but to Mike, she whispered 'I'll tell you all about it later'.

Chapter 16

Whilst Sally had been sorting Hannah out, the others had ordered another couple of bottles of Prosecco, so she was now playing catch up. After another couple of glasses, she was starting to feel really hungry and more than a little bit tipsy.

'OK then, who's up for hitting the buffet. I'm bloody starving and if I don't soak some of this alcohol up soon I'm going to fall over!'

No-body needed asking twice and they all finished their drinks and made their way up to the buffet.

None of them had stayed awake long enough to make the midnight buffet before but they were glad they had tonight as it was a sight to behold. There were the usual burgers, hotdogs and chips but there was also a nacho station, complete with bowls of cheese, jalapenos, salsa and sour cream, a pick your own toppings, pizza station, a curry station with 3 different types of curry, rice, nans, poppadums' and various chutneys and an assortment of sandwiches and rolls. But the main attraction had to be the enormous chocolate fountain surrounded by bowls of fruit, marshmallows, churros and fudge for dipping, as well as platters of chocolate gateaux, cheesecake, tarts, profiteroles, brownies and bowls of chocolate mousse. In fact anything that could have been covered in chocolate, had been.

Sally headed straight for the chocolate fountain but Mike managed to steer her away from it.

'I think perhaps you'd better have something savoury before you go head first into that Sal. Otherwise I think you're going to be as sick as a dog!'

'Oh, OK. I'll go and get myself some nachos, or shall I have a curry. See, now I don't know what to have. What are you having?'

'I might get a curry with all the trimmings. If you get a big plate of nachos we can share'

'Sounds like a plan' said Sally grabbing a plate and heading towards the nacho station.

Once they had all loaded up with food and found a table, the conversation took a bit of a back seat as everyone was tucking in to their supper.

'Blimey, I didn't realise I were this hungry' said Valerie, getting to grips with a massive piece of pizza. 'But then we do normally have our dinner at about 8.30, so this is well overdue!'

'Too right it is' said Simon, in between mouthfuls of chicken curry, 'I haven't eaten anything since about 4 o'clock this afternoon and it's gone midnight now, that's over 8 hours without food. It's a wonder I'm not wasting away!'

'Really!' laughed Candice. 'So the tube of Pringles and packet of biscuits that you demolished before we came out tonight doesn't count then!'

'Oh, I forgot about them. But they were only snacks to help soak up the alcohol so no, they don't really count!'

After they had finished their supper, they all took it in turns to visit the chocolate fountain. Sally came back laden down with a piece of pretty much everything.

'If you eat all that Sal, you are going to be up all night being sick, and I'm not clearing up after you!'

'Don't be a spoilsport Mike, I won't be sick and even if I am, it will have been worth it! I'm on holiday and I'm going to treat myself. It's not like I eat like this at home is it?'

Sally dived into her chocolate feast, completely ignoring the looks she was getting from Mike, who, for once, had been quite sparing with his dessert, having only come back with one piece of cheesecake and a couple of chocolate dipped marshmallows.

'I think that maybe your eyes are bigger than your belly young lady' exclaimed Anton as he watched Sally struggle with a large piece of chocolate gateaux. 'Admit defeat my dear, no-one will hold it against you!'

'You're right' admitted Sally as she pushed her plate away from her, 'I've had it. If I eat another mouthful I'm going to explode'

'Told you!' laughed Mike. 'She's like this all the time when it comes to chocolate, just can't help herself!'

'I must admit it is all rather lovely' said Anton finishing up his mousse, 'but I couldn't eat too much of it as I think I would be up half the night. This is just enough for me.'

'So, is anyone up for a nightcap in the bar?' asked Valerie, wiping the tell-tale signs of a chocolate covered churros from her mouth.

'We might just come in for half an hour until this lot has gone down' said Mike, patting his stomach. 'I think Sally could definitely do with a black coffee!'

'Don't know what you mean. I'm absolutely fine. In fact I've never been better' slurred Sally, who was starting to look a little bit jaded.

They all made their way back down to the bar and ordered coffees and brandies, although Sally just stuck to the coffee as she had already had far too much booze! While they were waiting for their drinks, Mike made his excuses and made off to the Gents. After a good 20 minutes he came back, looking more than a bit pleased with himself.

'Oh please don't tell me you've made another friend in the toilets' laughed Sally, 'you'll be getting a bit of a reputation at this rate!'

'No, as I was walking round, I passed the Casino and just quickly poked my nose in to have a look. I can't believe we haven't been in there, it looks really nice, there was a duo singing in the bar area who were quite good. Anyway, I spotted Rick and his wife at the bar so I went over, introduced myself and thanked him for all the information I managed to get from his forums. I bought them both a drink and just stood having a natter. They are a really lovely couple, I'll introduce you to them if we manage to see them again. Right, I'd better get some more coffees in as mine's gone cold now!'

Mike ordered another round of coffee and brandies and then, one by one, they started to make their way back to their cabins.

'So, what was all that about this evening with Hannah?' asked Mike as they were getting ready for bed.

'Oh blimey, I forgot about that. She hasn't got an eating disorder after all, she's pregnant!'

'No way! Is she pleased? I must admit, Richard never said anything to me'

'That's because he doesn't know' said Sally and proceeded to tell Mike what Hannah had told her.

'So, I think perhaps its best we keep it to ourselves for now, until she tells him and they either make an announcement or they don't'

'Absolutely' agreed Mike. 'My lips are sealed, now turn that bloody light off, I'm knackered!'

Chapter 17

The next day was at sea and it gave them a chance to catch up on some sunbathing. No-one had made any plans and they were all just going to do their own thing which, for some of them, included nursing hangovers! Sally had, as Mike predicted, been as sick as a dog when she got back to the cabin and although this wasn't pleasant at the time, it did meant that she had no hangover. Mike, on the other hand, had a banging headache and woke up in desperate need of some stodge!

After a full English and several cups of coffee, he was starting to feel a bit more human and both he and Sally spent the rest of the day on deck topping up their tans, ready for that evenings' formal dinner.

They had, the previous evening, arranged to meet up with everyone in the Artemis bar before all sharing a table in the main dining room. As it would be a 5 course gala dinner that night, all they had for lunch was a sandwich from the pool bar as they didn't want to spoil their appetite. After a full day's sun, and feeling nice and relaxed, they went back to the cabin to get ready.

'I wonder what happened with Richard and Hannah?' asked Mike as he struggled to get to grips with his cummerbund.

'Oh, I don't know. I hope she told him about the baby. I haven't seen them anywhere today so I assume everything went OK. I'm sure we'll find out something tonight. Now, do you want me to do that thing up for you or are you going to struggle all night?'

Once they were all dressed up, Sally took a selfie of them both in their finery to put on Facebook. They both looked resplendent in their outfits. Sally had on a long blue, silk dress that hung in all the right places and looked amazing with her tan. She had straightened her hair and the blonde highlights from the sun made it look like spun gold. She certainly didn't look as though she would be 50 in a couple of days' time. Mike had on his black Tuxedo, this time with silver bow tie and matching cummerbund and with his golden tan and sun bleached hair, they made a good looking couple.

'Wow' said Mike looking at his wife appreciatively. 'You scrub up well, don't you?'

'I'll take that as a compliment, shall I?' laughed Sally. 'You don't look too bad yourself actually'

'No I don't do I' said Mike, preening himself in the mirror.

'Right enough of that, let's go and meet the others. I'm looking forward to tonight. I love these formal nights.'

As they passed through the Atrium, they decided to have another picture taken by the ship's photographer, as the previous one had turned out so well. By the time they had finished getting themselves into numerous poses, to achieve that perfect look for the camera, and then walked back round the Atrium to get to the bar, they were the last ones to get there.

Hannah and Richard were sitting with the others and Sally tried to catch her attention but to no avail. It was difficult to gage by their expressions what had happened so Sally decided to leave them until they were ready to spill the beans.

After a quick G & T they all headed off to the dining room to wait for a table that would accommodate all eight of them. They were seated quickly and in no time at all waiters started serving the lavish 5 course dinner. Now that the misunderstanding about Simon was out of the way, everyone seemed to get on like they had been lifelong friends, and the conversation flowed like a vintage wine.

As always, the food was sumptuous and the service impeccable.

Just before dessert was served, the wine waiter appeared with a couple of bottles of Champagne in ice buckets, complete with crystal flutes for them all.

'What's this all in aid of then?' asked Anton, looking at Sally. 'It's not your birthday yet, is it?'

'No, not until Wednesday. Perhaps it's from the Captain?' said Sally looking equally bemused.

After the wine waiter ensured that everyone had a full glass of bubbly, Richard tapped his glass with his spoon to get their attention.

'You may have notice that we disappeared a bit sharpish last night after Hannah had been to the ladies with Sally to "get something out of her eye". Well, as Sally will know, she didn't have anything in her eye at all but had confided in her that she was worried about telling me something in case I was angry. Well, tell me she did, thanks to Sally for guiding her in the right direction, and I couldn't have been less angry if I tried. In fact I was bloody over the moon and I can now share it with all of you. Hannah and myself are going to be proud parents as she is about 3 months pregnant.'

Everyone round the table gave them a round of applause, raised a glass and congratulated them but they all wanted to know why on earth Hannah thought Richard would be angry.

'Well, as most of you know, we always said that we didn't want children and I think, at one point in the past, I may have commented that it was the best decision that I ever made. I always thought that Hannah was completely against it so I never really broached the subject again but I think in my heart of hearts I always thought that if it happened one day, I wouldn't have been too upset. So, when Hannah thought she was going through the menopause and got pregnant, she thought I would be outraged and even thought about a termination at one point, although she said she could never have gone through with it. When she finally told me last night, I was over the moon.'

Sally looked at Hannah and she was beaming, in fact she looked like a completely different person to the sobbing mess that she was last night.

'I'm just so happy that Richard wants this baby as much as I do' said Hannah, patting her belly. 'I can't believe I ever thought he wouldn't. But now I can really start to enjoy this cruise instead of worrying. I've even seen the ships doctor who has given me something for the sickness so at least I can start eating some of this fabulous food now, and hopefully I can be less of a miserable old cow and join in the fun!'

'Oh my God' exclaimed Richard looking mortified, 'there's us going on about having a baby and I didn't even think about how it would make you two feel' he said to Simon and Candice.

'Oh don't be so silly Richard' said Candice, 'we're over the moon for both of you and we're way past having the screaming ab dabs every time someone mentions the "B" word. Just you make sure you invite us to the Christening!'

'That goes without saying' said Hannah, 'in fact you're all invited as I'm sure we will all be staying in touch long after this cruise finishes.'

Hannah winked at Sally and mouthed a 'thank you'. Sally was just glad that everything had turned out for the best. She loved a happy ending.

They all carried on drinking Champagne, and chatting about Richard and Hannah's good news for a short while then had relatively early nights as they were all desperate to see Santorini come into view early the next morning!

Chapter 18

Sally and Mike had set their alarm for 6.30 so they could sit on the balcony and watch the sunrise as the ship sailed into the bay surrounding Santorini. They woke just before the alarm went off and quickly threw on some clothes, grabbing the cameras and a couple of mugs of coffee before they sat on the balcony to watch the scenery. They weren't disappointed.

'Oh my God, look at that view. It's absolutely stunning isn't it?' said Mike turning his camcorder on and panning around the caldera as it got closer. 'You do realise that this bay we are sailing into is actually the world's largest volcanic crater.'

'Yeah, but didn't that big explosion happen donkey's years ago? It's not like its active or anything now is it?'

'Yes it is' Mike informed her. 'Even though it erupted over 3,000 years ago, the Thera volcano is still active. I vaguely remember seeing a programme on the History channel about it. Some divers went there recently to have a look and it is definitely still a bit lively down there. In fact, if you can see those two tiny islands over there as we are coming into the bay, well they are a result of the last underwater eruption in 1950. I don't think we've got anything to worry about today, but you never can tell!'

'Thanks for that' said Sally peering over the side. 'Oh well, there's nothing we can do if it blows, so not much point in worrying about it is there? It is a beautiful place though. Isn't this where they reckon the lost island of Atlantis is?'

'So a lot of people believe. It would be nice to think it was down there somewhere, wouldn't it?'

'Yeah, it would' agreed Sally. 'So, where's the main town on the island then?'

'Right up there' pointed Mike craning his neck, 'at the top of those cliffs in front of us'

'Really! How the bloody hell are you supposed to get up there then?'

'Ah, funny you should mention that' said Mike delving into his trusty cruise booklet. 'It says here that there are three ways to get there. You can go up by cable car, which goes every 20 minutes and costs about 5 euros or you can go on a mule ride, along the pathways that you can just see over there, that's about 8 euros I think. Or you can walk the same path as the mules but it's up around 600 steps, so not for the fainthearted! I think perhaps we'll go on the cable car, unless of course you fancy walking!'

'I think not!' said Sally looking horrified. 'I'm not even sure I fancy the cable car but it's either that or sit on some poor donkey and I'm definitely not doing that. Poor little things, it's not right to use them like that'.

'No, I know, but it's what's been done for hundreds of years and it's not going to suddenly change just because a few tourists object to it. So, cable car it is then. I'm getting quite excited now!'

'I'm not sure we'll be going anywhere to be honest' said Sally looking worried. 'The ships stopped and it looks like we've dropped anchor!'

'Oh, I forgot to mention that. We have to get a tender to shore as there's not a port terminal on Santorini!'

'You really are full of surprises aren't you Mike!'

'Well, I did tell you to read the information booklet the travel agent sent through about all the ports of call. It really is interesting and you don't get any nasty surprises that way! Now, if you hurry up and get ready, we can pop into the buffet and have a bit of breakfast before we get on the tender'

They finished getting dressed and putting their stuff together and then made their way down to the buffet restaurant, where they managed to get a seat, even though it was already heaving with people who obviously had the same idea as them. They had a light breakfast of some cereal and a couple of slices of toast as well as a jug of freshly brewed coffee. Sally also wrapped up a couple of Danish pastries and put them in her bag, for later! As they were leaving the restaurant, they bumped into Richard and Hannah who were also heading towards the disembarkation point for the tender to take them to Santorini.

'I take it you're going ashore then' asked Richard as they made their way down the corridor to the lifts.

'Absolutely, this is the one island I've really been looking forward to seeing. I can't wait to get on there and have a look around. What about you two? If you've got nothing planned, why don't you tag along with us? We haven't got any trips booked or anything, we're just going to go where the mood takes us.'

'As long as you don't mind, that would be really lovely' said Hannah 'I will have to go up by cable car though as I don't think a pregnant woman on a donkey is a good idea!'

'Obviously not a big fan of the Nativity then?' laughed Mike

'Trust you' groaned Sally shaking her head, 'No, it's alright we'll be going by cable car as well. I just think it's cruel to sit on donkeys and make them walk miles up mountains.'

'Oh don't get her started about cruelty to animals, we'll be here all day! Right, come on Mary and Joseph, let's get on this tender before the hordes come down from the buffet!'

They all walked down to where disembarkation was taking place and got onto the first tender of the morning. It was only a short trip over to the small harbour and once there, they found a few bars and restaurants as well as some shops selling souvenirs and traditional local products. This would also be where they would take their chosen method of transport up to the main town. There were a few people from their ship that had decided to make the steep climb by donkey and Sally glared and tutted at them as they went past them on their journey. They spent half an hour or so looking round a couple of the shops and then strolled over to where they picked up the cable car. Luckily there wasn't a massive queue and it wasn't long before they were high above the harbour and well on their way to the top of the cliff, which Mike informed them was approximately 260 meters above sea level!

It wasn't a terribly long journey, which was just as well as Sally was starting to feel a little woozy.

'You not brilliant with heights then Sal' asked Richard, who was loving every minute of the cable car ride.

'Not that good, no' said Sally, staring at the top of the cliff and willing it to get nearer. 'I'll be alright when I get up there, I just don't like the thought of dangling in mid-air like this!'

The rest of them however were drinking in the breath taking views of the bay and the two massive cruise ships that had just anchored next to theirs.

They finally reached their destination and Sally breathed a sigh of relief.

'Oh, thank God that's over. I think I might have to walk back down!'

'OK love, but you'll be walking on your own I'm afraid' laughed Mike.

'But I might get trampled on by rabid donkeys!'

'You've changed your tune Sal. You were going to save the poor creatures from a life of drudgery half an hour ago, now they're just rabid! Now, what on earth are you two cackling about?' asked Mike as Richard and Hannah suddenly started shrieking with laughter.

'Oh my word. I've seen it all now' laughed Richard 'Have a look at who's coming up the donkey trail!'

They all looked over to where Richard was pointing and there was Anton, sitting astride a very rabid looking donkey who was trotting along as if he was auditioning for a part in Shrek. Anton was being thrown around like a rag doll and looked decidedly green around the gills. They all started waving and shouting to him and when he eventually made it to the top they ran over to him as he looked like he needed more than a helping hand getting off the creature.

'I do believe that was one of the worst experiences of my life' said Anton as he tried to regain his composure once he was on solid ground. 'I don't suppose anyone has got any anti-bacterial gel or wipes have they? Only I stink of, God only knows what and I dread to think what diseases I may have picked up along the way. This was definitely not one of my better ideas'

'Why on earth didn't you come on the cable car with us?' asked Sally, handing him a wet wipe. 'We didn't even think you were coming ashore today otherwise we would have waited for you.'

'No, I wasn't originally going to but then I thought, this is exactly the sort of thing that Kenny would have loved so I took the bull by the horns, or in this case the donkey by the ears, and made the epic journey up here. I do think I will be going back down by cable car though, my backside must be black and blue and I honestly don't think I'll be able to sit down for a week!'

'Oh bless you' said Sally taking him by the arm and leading him away from the donkeys. 'I think what you need is a nice coffee with just the merest hint of brandy in it, so let's go and find a bar!'

They all headed off into the maze of blue and white that was Fira, the capital of Santorini. There were bars, restaurants and shops galore, all nestled in the quaint cobbled streets that weaved through the town. Some of them had various levels of patios and balconies to make the most of the space that they had and all of them had views to die for. It really was a stunning place, and everyone agreed it was the best that they had seen yet. The only downside they could think of, was the amount of people that were milling about. In fact there were hordes of tourists still spilling out from the many cruise ships that were now docked in the bay below, all of them headed upwards to Fira.

'As stunning as it is, I'm not over sure I'd want to stay here' said Richard holding on to Hannah and desperately trying to stop her from being pushed over by the hundreds of people frantically trying to get past them. 'I can honestly say that I've never seen so many people gathered in one place'.

'Yeah it is a bit manic' admitted Mike, 'but I suppose that's the price you pay for going to somewhere as stunning as this, everyone has the same idea. I would imagine that if you're staying here, you breathe a sigh of relief around 5 o'clock when the cruise ships all depart'.

They carried on getting jostled around for another hour or so until Richard managed to find them a little taverna hidden away down a maze of alleyways. It was like a calming oasis after the noise and crowds of the main town and they just hoped that they would be able to find their way back again!

The taverna had the most stunning views of Santorini bay and the five of them sat in awe of their surroundings drinking freshly squeezed orange juice, or in Anton's case, coffee and a large brandy, and munching on delicious little spring rolls that were stuffed with sundried tomatoes, mint and the local chloro cheese, which was very similar to Feta, just a bit milder.

'Oh my word, just look at that view' sighed Hannah, 'I don't think it couldn't get any better than this, could it?'

'Nope you're absolutely right' agreed Sally 'It makes you glad to be alive on days like this'

'Yes, I suppose it was worth the trip from hell just to get up here and see this' admitted Anton, grudgingly, as he sat back, albeit tentatively, and took in the stunning views.

Chapter 19

They sat chatting and admiring the views for another half an hour or so before making their way back out to the crowded streets of Fira for a bit more sightseeing and shopping before lunch. Sally and Hannah were enjoying some girlie chat and window shopping whilst the boys lagged behind, when suddenly a young lad, who had been behind them whilst they were gazing into a bakery window, suddenly grabbed Hannah's bag from off her shoulder. She tried to get it off him but he was a lot stronger than her and she ended up being thrown to the ground whilst he legged it into the crowds. Sally shouted out to the boys, who were a few yards behind and while her and Richard helped Hannah back to her feet, Mike and Anton made off to try and catch the thief.

Although Hannah seemed OK, apart from a grazed knee from where she fell, and feeling a bit shaken, Richard and Sally were really concerned for her seeing as she was pregnant. The owner of the bakery that they were looking in at the time, came running out as he had seen what had happened. He brought Hannah inside the shop, sat her down and got her a cold drink.

Richard introduced himself to the bakery owner, who in turn introduced himself as Nikos, and explained that Hannah was pregnant. He asked if there was a hospital nearby where they could go and get Hannah checked out. Nikos told him that he could get a taxi for him to take him to the hospital but he would have to be prepared for a long wait once he got there. Hannah was adamant that she was OK and didn't want to go to hospital.

'I'll be fine Richard, stop fussing. As soon as we get back on board ship, I'll go and see the ship's Doctor and he can examine me. If we go off to the hospital now, chances are we'll miss the ship and that would be a bloody nightmare.'

'OK, if you're sure? As soon as Mike and Anton get back, we'll head over to where the cable car station is. Actually, talk of the devil, here they come now.'

'Flipping hell, I'm not sure who needs medical treatment more, me or Anton' laughed Hannah as Mike walked into the shop with a very red and puffed out Anton, who was holding his sides.

'I honestly didn't think I was this unfit' he wheezed, 'It's the gym for me when I get home I think!'

'It was worth it though' said Mike handing Hannah her bag. 'Anton was like a rat up a drainpipe running down there. He caught up with the thieving little scroat and grabbed the bag back. Unfortunately, he got away but he only looked about 10. A right little Artful Dodger! Anyway, how are you Hannah?'

'I'm fine thanks Mike and thank you Anton for getting my bag back for me. There wasn't a lot of money in there but it did have my camera and the photos on there are irreplaceable. Honestly, you wouldn't think that sort of thing could happen somewhere as idyllic has this would you?'

'Unfortunately, we have seen quite a bit of this recently' said Nikos. 'We think it is gypsies coming over from the mainland. It's easy pickings with the crowds and with tourists every day from the cruise ships. All we can say to people is that they don't advertise they have money, so don't wear flash jewellery or carry expensive cameras and phones. Perhaps wear a money belt or carry a bag across the body. I know you shouldn't have to worry about such things but unfortunately it is a sign of the times. Hopefully they will tire of Santorini soon and move on but until then we just have to be alert!'

Hannah and Richard thanked Nikos for his kindness and then the five of them walked back to the cable car, despite Richard's pleas that Hannah get a taxi, even though it was only a 5 minute walk. There was only a short queue for the next trip down and in no time at all they were stepping onto a tender to take them back on board ship.

'You really didn't all have to come back to the ship with me' said Hannah to the others. 'I could have quite easily come back on my own. I feel awful that you've missed out on seeing more of the island. You didn't even get to have lunch!'

'No, but look at what the guy who owned the bakery gave us' said Anton opening the bag he was carrying and showing them a selection of delicious looking pastries.

'Really! He gave us all that. What a lovely bloke' said Mike, reaching into the bag to grab himself something to eat!

'Oh no you don't' said Anton, slapping him on the wrist. 'These are for when we get back on board. I thought we could find a quiet corner somewhere, get some coffees and then have them. I'm sure you can wait a few more minutes.'

'OK if I must. Oh and don't worry Hannah I think we were all pretty much ready to head back anyway. Those crowds were really starting to get to me. You just couldn't walk around and look at things without constantly bumping into someone. At least we saw quite a bit of the town and those amazing views'

'Yes, and thanks to you and Anton I've still got my camera to remind me of them. The coffees are all on me when we get back'

Very soon they were all back on board and sitting on the prom deck waiting for Anton to hand out the goodies while Hannah ordered some coffees to be brought to them. Richard begged Hannah to go straight to the ships Doctor but she was having none of it and finally convinced him to wait until they had had a bite to eat. The coffees arrive and everyone tucked into the delicious home-made pastries that the shop owner had so kindly bagged up for them.

'These are really gorgeous' said Hannah licking her lips and trying to stop the flaky pastry from her cheese and spinach pie from going everywhere. 'They're almost worth getting mugged for!'

'Don't even joke about that' scolded Richard. 'Right, you've had a bite to eat, now can we go and see the ship's Doctor to get you checked out?'

'Oh, OK' said Hannah wearily. 'If I must. I'm sure there's nothing wrong though, I feel absolutely fine and it's going to cost an absolute fortune having anything medical done on the ship!'

'I know, but it will be worth it just to know you and our baby are both OK. Now come on, finish your coffee and let's get going.'

Hannah gulped down the last of her Latte and followed Richard inside, stopping briefly to find out what time everyone was meeting for dinner that evening.

'It's one thing after another on this trip' said Mike. 'You could never say we had a boring holiday could you?'

'No it's definitely not boring, that's for sure' agreed Sally. 'I just hope Hannah is OK, but I'm sure the ship's Doctor will look after her. Right, who's up for a G & T before we go back?'

After a couple of drinks on the sun deck whilst watching the ship sail away from yet another Greek island, the three of them retired to their respective cabins to get ready for the evening meal.

Sally and Mike didn't want a late one that night as they were going on a trip when they docked in Crete. They had booked a taxi to take them to Elounda so they could get the ferry across to the island of Spinalonga and were both really looking forward to it. They were going to meet everyone in the bar for a couple of cocktails and then go off and have a meal on their own in the Grill so they could have a relatively early night.

Just as they were ready to leave the cabin, someone knocked on the door. When Sally opened it, she was greeted by Richard and Hannah.

'Hiya Sally, we were just passing your door on the way to the bar and thought we'd knock for you'

'That's very thoughtful of you Richard' laughed Sally. 'Now what's the real reason you two are standing there? Everything's alright with the baby isn't it?'

'Well let's put it this way, I'm glad I got checked out' said Hannah, looking serious.

'No, what's happened?' said Sally and Mike in unison, both looking really concerned.

'Oh don't worry, there's nothing wrong, it's just we went there with concern for the baby and it turns out there are babies. We're having twins!'

'Twins!' exclaimed Mike. 'Blimey, they're like buses, wait ages for one then two come along together!'

'I suppose you're right Mike. It was a bit of a shock, I can tell you, but Richard is over the moon, aren't you love?'

'Yeah, I still can't get my head around having one baby, let alone two. It really is the best news ever. Now let's get to the bar and tell the others.'

They met Anton, Simon and Candice, who were already in the bar and Mike bought everyone a drink to celebrate Hannah and Richard's news. Candice said that she had just seen Valerie who was off to meet some friends and would meet them all later. Hannah said she would either see her later and tell her the news or leave a message on her cabin phone.

After another couple of drinks Sally and Mike made their excuses and went off to the Grill restaurant to have a meal and then get an early night ready for their excursion the next day, leaving the others ordering yet more cocktails. They had a lovely meal and were back in their cabin, and ready for bed, by 10 o'clock.

Chapter 20

The next morning they were up and showered by 7.30. Sally had packed the bags that they would be taking out with them, the night before, so once dressed they went off to the restaurant where they had a leisurely full English to set them up for the day. Their taxi was ordered for 9.30 so, as soon as breakfast was finished, they made their way down to where everyone was disembarking. As soon as they stepped onto the quayside they saw a taxi driver holding up a placard with Mr and Mrs Edwards on it. Once inside the air-conditioned cab, they sat back, relaxed and looked forward to the hour or so's drive to Elounda.

It was a lovely drive, taking in stunning coastal views as well some very picturesque villages. They drove through the party town of Malia, which at that time in the morning was quite deserted, given that the revellers had all probably just got in from the previous night, and also Agios Nikolaos where they would be stopping on the way back. As they got nearer to Elounda, they could see Spinalonga in the distance. The boat that would be taking them over to the island was leaving in about 20 minutes so they had plenty of time to get there, but even if they missed that one, they sailed every half an hour so there was no real rush.

The taxi dropped them off as near to where the boat was moored as possible and they arranged to meet him back at the same place in a couple of hours. The boat was certainly no pleasure cruiser but it did the job of getting them over to the island. Luckily it wasn't a very long journey, as Mike was convinced that the boat wouldn't last many more crossings, and they all managed to get off in one piece. Once everyone had re-found their land legs, they started the tour around the island.

Although Spinalonga had various roles and uses throughout the centuries, it is for the leper colony that the island is most remember for. From 1913 the colony served the whole of Greece and hundreds of lepers lived and died on the island, separated from friends and families on the mainland by just a narrow strip of water. In July 1957 the last remaining sufferers were transferred to a hospital near Athens and in 1970 the ghost town of run-down streets and houses was declared a protected archaeological site. Nowadays, Spinalonga is the third most visited archaeological site behind the Acropolis and Knossos with thousands of tourists visiting it each year.

Sally and Mike walked the cobbled streets, amazed at how people could overcome such adversity and come together to build a community with its own rules and values, all from run down streets and houses that were abandoned by Turkish occupants at the end of the previous century. The only downside was the crowds of people visiting the island at any given time meaning you had to pretty much go round in a one-way system and not wander off and take your time exploring, which Sally and Mike had hoped they could do.

'It doesn't matter where we seem to go lately, there seems to be a million other people tagging along!' laughed Sally. 'It would be nice to go somewhere and have the place to ourselves'.

'Don't think that's going to happen babe, these places are so popular I reckon the only time you'll get to be alone is if you visit around midnight! But at least we are seeing something of Greece and, to be fair, even with the crowds this place is pretty amazing, isn't it?'

'It certainly is' agreed Sally. 'I must admit, I've always had a hankering to see this place after reading that novel "The Island". You should read it sometime, it really brings the island to life and you can just imagine what it was like years ago when those poor people were banished here.'

'Yeah, might give it a go when we get home if you've still got it. Right, it looks like we're back to where we started so I suppose we've got to get back on that old rust bucket of a boat again. Thank God it's only a 15 minute journey back!'

They got on the boat with the rest of the sightseers and endured the nail biting journey back to Elounda. They still had a few minutes until the taxi came back for them so they popped into the nearest café for a couple of bottles of water and to use the loo. By the time they had paid, their taxi was pulling up so they got back into the air-conditioned car ready for the short ride to Agios Nikolaos.

Agios Nikolaos, or Ag Nik as it is more commonly known, was only a 20 minute taxi ride away and, as it was on their way back to the ship, they decided they would spend a couple of hours there, having heard great things about the place from Simon and Candice who had been there a couple of years ago. They weren't disappointed as the taxi took them round to the harbour and the inland lake that is connected to the sea. Before he dropped them off, the driver told them that legend has it that the lake is bottomless so not to fall in or they would never be found again!

'I have actually read that' said Mike as they walked round to find a restaurant. 'At one time, they actually thought it may have been connected to the lost island of Atlantis, but I think they have actually proved now it's not actually bottomless but it is extremely deep. It's also where the goddess Athena bathed, again according to legend'

'There's an awful lot of legends going on here. But then I suppose we are in Greece, the land of legends!'

'I suppose we are' agreed Mike 'Right, enough about legends. I don't know about you but I could eat a scabby dog'

'Not sure about that' said Sally 'But I could definitely eat a plate of calamari and a glass of something cold.'

They found a restaurant overlooking the fabled lake and ordered a couple of plates of calamari, a Greek salad and a carafe of red wine. After having a leisurely lunch and a spot of people watching, they only had about 40 minutes to have a look round before the taxi took them back to Elounda. They walked around the harbour and took some pictures before meeting the taxi at the agreed pick up point.

Just over an hour later they pulled into the harbour at Elounda where the Grecian Princess sat waiting for them. After paying the taxi driver and giving him a well-deserved tip, they joined the queue of passengers waiting to board the ship.

'It's a shame it's not a late sailing from here tonight' said Sally 'I wouldn't have minded having a look round Elounda, but we've just run out of time again.'

'Oh well, we'll just have to come back to Crete again sometime' laughed Mike. 'Isn't that Simon and Candice up front? I thought they were staying on board today for a bit of sunbathing!'

'Yep, it's definitely them all right' agreed Sally waving frantically trying to catch their attention. 'I think Simon is trying to mime, he'll meet us in the bar'

The queue soon went down and within a few minutes they were joining Simon and Candice in the bar. After getting in a round of drinks, Simon suggested they sit down at a table by the window.

Sally told them both about their trip to Spinalonga and Ag Nik and asked them what they had been up to.

'Well, you're never going to believe what we've done today' said Candice, looking really pleased with herself. 'We've only gone and adopted a puppy. She'll be ready for us in a few weeks' time, after she's had all her inoculations and been spayed'

'Oh my God' exclaimed Sally. 'Where on earth did you get a puppy from?'

'From a place on the other side of the island. There's this Greek guy who's got a shelter and devotes his life to saving stray dogs. He's got loads of them of all ages and although he tries to re-home the dogs, he does end up keeping quite a lot of them. Anyway, I've been following him on Facebook for months and I pestered Simon to take me to see him. We did originally only plan on making a fuss of all the dogs, giving a donation and handing out some treats and toys that we had bought with us, but we ended up falling in love with one of the pups that he'd recently rescued. She's a 9 week old Lurcher cross called Lara and she is absolutely adorable. I can't wait until we get her home!'

'Don't you get any ideas' said Mike as he saw Sally's eyes light up. 'We're both at work all day, it wouldn't be fair!'

'Aren't you forgetting something babe? I've given up work, so there's really no excuse for us not to have a dog now. I wish we were here for another day so I could go and see this shelter'

'Well we're not unfortunately but if you really are serious about getting a dog perhaps we can go and look at one of the shelters in Cyprus next time we visit Lucy. She's always saying how desperate they are for people to give their strays a home. It's something to think about when we get home'

'Really!' exclaimed Sally excitedly. 'Can we book our flights as soon as we get home?'

'Oh no, I've done something now haven't I?' groaned Mike. 'I'm likely never to hear the last of this now, until we go to Cyprus.'

'No, you're so not' laughed Sally. 'So, did either of you take any pictures of little Lara then?'

Candice scrolled down her phone and showed Sally some pictures of her new puppy who was, as she had said earlier, absolutely adorable.

By the time they had gone through Candice's many pictures of Lara and finished their drinks it was getting on for 6 o'clock.

'Blimey, look at the time' said Simon glancing at his watch. 'We'd better get back and start getting ready for tonight, you know how long it takes these two to get ready! We're eating in the buffet tonight if you want to join us. We don't normally go in there for dinner but they've got a Chinese night tonight and I could kill for a chow mein!'

'Oh, that sounds good' said Mike 'We both love Chinese food. In fact we were only saying yesterday how much we fancied some, so yes we'd love to join you. Shall we meet in the Artemis as usual?'

'No, I tell you what, let's have a drink in the pool bar for a change, it's right next door to the buffet restaurant. We can always go to the Artemis after dinner for a couple. About 8 o'clock do you?'

'Perfect, see you then'

The four of them went back to get showered and changed and met back at the pool bar just after 8 o'clock for a couple of cocktails, before completely gorging themselves on Chinese food from the buffet. When they had finished eating, they strolled round the promenade deck to try and walk off some of their dinner, before ending up in the Artemis Bar for some coffees. They had just sat down and ordered when Anton appeared and plonked himself next to Candice who started showing him pictures of her new puppy. After a few minutes he came over to Sally and gave her a hug.

'Sorry sweetie, I didn't mean to ignore you, I was just dying to see the pictures of little Lara, and what a darling she is!'

'She is gorgeous isn't she?' agreed Sally 'And Mike has said we can have dog now that I'm not at work, so I'll be booking a flight to Cyprus when we get home to have a look at the strays out there! Have you seen Richard and Hannah or Valerie on your travels?'

'I saw Valerie earlier and she said she was meeting some friends and I think Richard and Hannah were booked into The Blue Room for a meal tonight. I'm sure we can all meet up tomorrow at some time. We've got two days at sea now so I'm sure we can have a late one!'

'Yeah that would be good' said Sally yawning. 'I don't think we will tonight though. All that sightseeing today has worn me out, I'm bloody knackered. I don't know about you Mike, but I'm ready to hit the sack!'

'I must admit, I am too. We must be getting old babe!'

And with that both Sally and Mike left the others in the bar and headed off to their cabin for a relatively early night!

Chapter 21

The next morning Sally woke to find Mike standing over her with a handful of presents and the cabin covered in banners and balloons.

'Happy Birthday babe. What does it feel like to finally reach that half a century?'

'Ha, ha, very funny. I don't think. I can't believe I'm 50. I feel so old now' Sally got out of bed and went over to the mirror to examine her face. 'Look, even more wrinkles have appeared overnight. That's it, my life will never be the same again and stop laughing, it's not funny!'

'Oh don't be so dramatic Sal' laughed Mike 'You know damm well you don't look 50 so stop hunting for wrinkles and get over here and open these presents.'

'Ooh you shouldn't have gone to all this trouble' said Sally, not meaning a single word of it, and starting to tear into the first present.

For the next 10 minutes or so, Sally opened a pile of presents and cards from Mike and various people back home. Mike had bought her a designer bag, with matching purse that she'd had her eye on from one of the shops on board ship, although how he'd managed to get them back to the cabin without her seeing it, she didn't know! He'd also got her a beautiful silver necklace and matching earrings from a very expensive shop in Lakeside and a bottle of her favourite perfume. Karen had bought her a beautiful silk pashmina and a voucher for her favourite clothes shop and Mike's parents had both given her money. She also had some euros from Lucy in Cyprus and a spa voucher to use on board ship from the girls who she used to work with.

'Wow, I can't believe how spoilt I've been' said Sally hugging Mike and thanking him for the gorgeous presents. 'Look at all these goodies. It's worth being 50 just to get all this'

'Yep, you've done really well. Don't forget to book that spa treatment though because we've only got another 3 days left on the cruise!'

'No way. Three days! You've got to be kidding me, that's gone far too quickly. That's it, we'll just have to book another one when we get home! Right, let me put this money and jewellery away, then I can have a shower and we can go and get some breakfast. Where shall we go, the buffet?'

'No, let's go to the main dining room today and be waited on' said Mike, handing Sally a cup of tea. 'It's not like we're going anywhere today so we can have a nice leisurely breakfast and then decide what we want to do from there'

'OK, that sounds like a good idea. I feel like being waited on today. If you can't be pandered to on your birthday, when can you?'

They both showered and got dressed and then went off to the Parthenon dining room to get some breakfast. When they got to the restaurant, Mike told the Maître d' their name and cabin number and he lead them through the restaurant to a table in the far corner. As they neared their table, Sally could see Anton, Valerie, Simon and Candice and Hannah and Richard already seated and when they saw her and Mike approaching they all burst into a rousing chorus of "Happy Birthday to you". Sally feigned horror and embarrassment but really she was over the moon that they were all there and remembered her big day.

'Here she is, the birthday girl. Come and get yourself sat down and have some Bucks Fizz' said Anton pouring her a drink.

'Oh, this is absolutely lovely' said Sally, taking in the table with the '50' and 'Birthday Girl' helium balloons, table confetti and banner on the glass wall behind where she was sitting. 'I can't believe how spoilt I've been today, thank you all so much for this'

'Our pleasure my dear' said Anton, placing a small, but beautifully wrapped box in front of her. 'Here you go Sally, happy birthday and I hope you'll remember me and this wonderful cruise every time you see this'

Sally opened the box and was astounded to see it was a ship charm to go on her bracelet.

'Anton, you shouldn't have. It's absolutely gorgeous and I will definitely think of you when I wear it. Thank you so much'

Then everyone else followed Anton's lead and placed their presents in front of Sally, wishing her all the best on her birthday. There was a bottle of Champagne from Simon and Candice, some wine and a gift box full of baklava from Valerie and a beautiful silver Greek key bracelet from Hannah and Richard. Sally was completely overwhelmed and thanked everyone profusely before getting down to the serious business of ordering breakfast.

'Honestly, I can't thank you all enough for all this' said Sally as she was attaching Anton's charm to her bracelet. 'I couldn't have asked for a better way to celebrate my 50th. It's been amazing so far'

'And it's not even 10 o'clock' piped up Richard, 'so you've still got another 14 hours of your birthday to celebrate yet!'

'Well, what are we waiting for' said Mike, calling the waiter over, 'I'll order some more Bucks Fizz and get this party started!'

After a full breakfast and a few more glasses of bubbly they all left the dining room and made their way into the atrium to decide what they were going to do with their day. Sally said she needed to book a treatment at the spa and Anton was going to a talk by his favourite author. Valerie was going off to meet up with her "friend" and the others were going to have a few hours round the pool and they would all meet up later for the barbeque lunch that was being held on the sun deck.

Sally and Mike made their way round to the Spa where Sally booked to have a facial and her nails re-done the following day then they went back to the cabin to change into their swimwear. After stopping off for a quick latte in the atrium, they joined Hannah, Richard, Candice and Simon around the pool. Anton appeared about an hour later, armed with a signed copy of the guest author's latest novel and they all spent the rest of the morning lazing around and jumping in and out of the pool to cool down. By the time Valerie appeared it was getting on for lunchtime and they all trooped upstairs to the sun deck where a massive barbeque was underway. After eating, what seemed like their own body weight in burgers, chicken and ribs, they went back down to their sunbeds, got under the umbrellas and all had at least 2 hours sleep, only waking up when the resident entertainment crew decided to deafen them with a rather bad Abba impersonation. At that point they all decided it was time to go back inside!

'I was having a lovely sleep before that mob starting screeching in my ear' said Sally yawning. 'I wouldn't mind if they even sounded like Abba!'

'From where I was sitting, they sounded more like cross between Jedward and Susan Boyle' said Richard rubbing his ears, 'not pleasant!'

'No, it really wasn't' agreed Sally. 'Right, I think I've had enough sun for one day so I'm going to go back, have a nice shower and then sit on the balcony with a cheeky glass of Pinot. I tell you something, I'm really going to miss doing that when I get home!'

'You and me both' said Candice, 'I think that's exactly what I'm going to do. Now, what are we doing tonight?'

'I think we'll leave that up to the birthday girl to decide' said Anton, 'where do you fancy eating tonight Sal?'

'Well, to be honest, I wouldn't mind eating in the main dining room tonight. I had a quick look at the menu this morning and it looks really good. If that's OK with everyone else?'

'Perfect' said Simon, 'shall we all meet for drinks in the Artemis bar at 7.30 and we'll book a table for about 8.30 on our way through to the bar'

'Yeah, sounds like a plan' agreed Mike, 'we'll see you all at 7.30 at the bar then.'

When Sally and Mike got back to their cabin, there was a bottle of Champagne on ice waiting for them, together with a card wishing Sally a happy birthday from the Shore Excursion Team.

'Oh that is so sweet' said Sally reading the card. 'I bet that's from Valerie's friend Fergus, she must have told him it was my birthday. We must stop off at the desk on the way to dinner and thank him. I think we'll put this in the fridge and have it tomorrow as I've got a feeling we'll have enough to drink tonight without this! That's what I meant to ask you, where on earth did those balloons and banners come from?'

'Ah, I brought them all from home and I was going to try and bribe our steward or someone to get them blown up but, as it happened, Richard and Hannah volunteered to take them when they went onshore in Crete as they needed to find a card shop anyway!'

'That was handy and thanks for bringing them, it was a lovely touch. I've had a brilliant day so far, considering I really wasn't looking forward to it. Now, what do you think of this dress? Not too revealing for an old lady is it?'

Sally and Mike were the last to arrive at the Artemis bar due to them stopping off at the Shore Excursion desk on the way so Sally could thank Fergus for the bottle of Champagne.

'Ah, here she comes at last' announced Anton, as Sally entered the bar, 'the Birthday girl, ensuring she's late to make a grand entrance!'

'No I'm not' said Sally 'I had to stop off at the front desk for something'

'I know sweetie, I'm only joking. But you do look rather divine tonight'

'Oh, what this old thing darling! Just something I found in the back of the cupboard and threw on' said Sally in her best Diva impersonation as she sashayed to the bar and ordered drinks for all her friends.

After a couple of drinks they all traipsed off to the dining room. The Maître 'd led them over to their normal table for 8 by the window which was, once again, resplendent in balloons and table confetti, this time all in a black and gold theme. There was also an ice bucket with 2 bottles of Champagne and a beautiful floral centrepiece.

'Oh my God' exclaimed Sally when she saw the table. 'This is beautiful. Your handiwork again, I assume Mike?'

'No, not this time, it's not. Karen e-mailed the ship and asked, as it was your 50th, if they could decorate the table for tonight. The Champagne's from me though!'

'Well, it's lovely' said Sally, admiring the centrepiece. 'I can't believe how spoilt I've been today. This really has been a fabulous birthday, thanks to you lot. Now let's get this Champagne opened!'

The evening passed far too quickly, as they savoured the delicious food, drank Champagne and talked about everything and anything. Before they knew it, they were finishing their coffees before being the last ones out of the restaurant. As they would still be at sea the following day and wouldn't need to get up early, they all made their way up to the main bar where the resident group was playing. They ordered some cocktails and carried on their conversations from dinner then the girls, and Anton, had a bit of a boogie when the group started playing some cheesy 80's music. By the time the music finished at around 1 o'clock in the morning, they were all knackered and ready for bed, especially Sally who was getting extremely unsteady on her feet and starting to slur her words, yet again!

'Thank you so much for tonight. I've had a wonderful birthday and I really love you all' said Sally as she hugged everyone before staggering off to her cabin, with Mike behind steering her in the right direction! Back in the cabin, Sally stripped off, went to the loo and half-heartedly took her make-up off. She then collapsed in bed and proceeded to snore her head off before Mike had even got out of his suit.

Chapter 22

The next morning saw quite a few hangovers, with Sally, Anton and Candice suffering the most. Some of them missed breakfast altogether but Sally decided that she desperately needed lots of strong coffee and some bacon sarnies. Her and Mike gingerly made their way down to the buffet restaurant where they found Anton sitting on his own, ploughing his way through a full English.
'God, you look like how I feel' groaned Sally as her and Mike plonked themselves down at Anton's table. Mike left Sally there while he went and loaded up on some rolls and a plate full of bacon. When he got back, there were mugs of steaming hot, black coffee on the table, which Sally had already dived into.
'Oh that's better. I needed that' sighed Sally as she took a large slurp of coffee. 'Never again, that's it. It's soft drinks for the rest of the cruise!'
'Yeah, right. I'll believe that when I see it. Bet you'll be on the gin again by tonight'
'You know me too well Mike' laughed Sally, piling bacon into one of the rolls that Mike had brought back.
'Actually, I'm glad I've met you this morning' said Anton. 'I wanted to ask you if you had any plans for tomorrow when we dock in Zakynthos.'
'No, not really' said Mike 'we were just going to have a walk round Zante Town and maybe get some lunch. Why, what did you have in mind?'
'Well, I've been to Zakynthos a few times now, on my own and with Kenny, and I always stay in the same hotel. Anyway, over the years we became firm friends with the owner and his family, even having them stay with us in London for a few days. So, I was wondering if you fancied coming with me to meet them and having some lunch in their fabulous restaurant.'

'That sounds brilliant' said Sally, now on her second bacon roll, 'we'd love to come with you. Thank you so much for asking us. I'll definitely be staying off the booze tonight then as I don't want to be hungover when we meet your friends'

'Don't forget it's our last formal night tonight' reminded Mike, 'and I think they are doing the Baked Alaska Parade as well.'

'What the bloody hell is that?' asked Sally.

'Well, seeing as you've asked' said Mike, who seemed to have become a mine of information on all things cruise related. 'It's a tradition on cruises that dates back over 100 years. It used to involve waiters parading through a darkened restaurant with a combination of fire and ice and has eventually evolved into them carrying trays of flaming Baked Alaskas. I think they are now paraded to that song "feeling hot, hot, hot". It's a shame but not many cruise lines seem to do it anymore, so the chance to see it is a real bonus!'

'Wow, that's definitely worth seeing. I'd better make sure I don't forget my phone tonight so I can video it!'

Once they'd had breakfast, the three of them went and found a shaded corner on the sun deck and settled down on their sunbeds. After they'd had a couple of hours sleep and some lunch they all started to feel back to normal again. They finished the day relaxing around the pool and then Sally went off for a couple of hours to have her facial and nails done. By the time they had gone back, showered and dressed in their finery, they were back to drinking cocktails in the bar, where they had all met up for that evenings' formal dinner.

'I see the no alcohol policy didn't take off then!' laughed Mike as Anton ordered another round of drinks.

'No, obviously not. But this is only my second and I think after some wine with dinner, I'll call it a day as we'll be docking quite early in the morning'

Once everyone had turned up, they all had one or two cocktails and then made their way into the restaurant where they enjoyed another fabulous 5 course gala dinner. The icing on the cake for the evening was indeed the Baked Alaska Parade which was a sight to behold, with teams of waiters walking through the restaurant with flaming desserts held aloft. Sally managed to video the whole thing, which she was really pleased about and it was the end to another perfect evening.

After they had finished their coffees, Anton and Sally and Mike took their leave and went back to their respective cabins for an early night. The others weren't far behind them as they had all had far too much the previous night and were looking forward to seeing land after a couple of days at sea.

Chapter 23

Sally and Mike were up around 6.30 the next morning and sat on the balcony to watch the ship sail into Zakynthos harbour. There wasn't a ripple on the sea and the haze that glistened over the land ahead promised a hot day ahead. Their breakfast arrived at just before 7 o'clock and they tucked into warm Danish pastries and mugs of hot coffee as the ship sailed nearer to port.

The ship finally docked at around 7.45 and they spent the next 45 minutes showering and getting ready, before heading off to meet Anton in the coffee shop. Anton was already waiting for them and they all ordered some coffee while waiting for disembarkation to begin at about 9 o'clock. As soon as the Captain announced which deck they would be disembarking from, they downed their coffees and made their way off the ship.

They walked through the port and out into the main town, where Anton said they would find a taxi and sure enough, a whole line of taxis stood waiting to be hailed. They jumped in the first one and Anton gave the driver the address of the hotel. The journey only took about 15 minutes so it wasn't long before they were pulling up outside Anton's friends' hotel in the small and friendly resort of Kalamaki.

The Ionian Dream was a small, family run hotel, owned by Christos and Anna Stephanidis, who, along with their daughter Eleni, son Petros, and their respective spouses, had made it into one of the most popular hotels on the island. It had just over 60 rooms which were all beautifully furnished in the typical Greek style of blue and white but came with extra touches, such as fresh flowers and bowls of fruit in every room and baskets of toiletries in the bathrooms. Along with the standard twin and double rooms, the hotel also had half a dozen suites with private gardens and whirlpools, and a separate honeymoon villa with a small private pool. The hotel also boasted a large bar, restaurant and separate breakfast room, along with a large pool set within well-manicured gardens, which included an area exclusively for weddings.

Christos and Anna were both in their 60s but neither of them looked their age and could keep up with even the youngest members of staff! They were a good looking couple, Christos was tall and well-built, although not fat, with a mass of greying hair and piercing blue eyes that sparkled when he smiled, which was most of the time as he was a very jovial person. Anna was tall like Christos but very willowy and elegant. She mainly wore her long dark hair up, secured with a stunning jewelled clip, and was always stylishly well dressed. With her graceful demeanour and elegant good looks she quite often reminded people of Audrey Hepburn, although after a few drinks she would let her hair down and party with the best of them!

The chic on-site restaurant was run by Eleni, who trained in New York under a top chef and who now served traditional Greek food with a twist, in comfortable and intimate surroundings. It had built up a great reputation and was enjoyed not only by guests of the hotel but also by Greek families who travelled from all over the island to eat there. Eleni's husband, Lambros worked the front of house in the restaurant and was extremely popular with all the guests as he was not only very good looking but also had the gift of the gab! Eleni on the other hand, who took after her father in looks, being quite heavy set, but extremely good looking with her father's piercing blue eyes and a mop of unruly hair, was rather quiet. Once she got to know someone, she would open up and show off the Stephanidis warmth and wit, but she was not very good around strangers and felt a lot more comfortable backstage in the kitchen, doing what she did best.

Petros, who took after his mother in looks but was loud and jovial like his father, was in charge of overseeing the bar staff and the hotel entertainment. His wife Anita, who was from England and met Petros when she came on holiday to Zante 20 years ago, organised the weddings that were held in the hotel. Petros helped his wife out when they got busy and it was something that they both really enjoyed doing, which was just as well as it was becoming more and more popular. In fact it was a wedding that they were all preparing for when Sally, Mike and Anton turned up.

'Oh my God, it's Anton' cried Christos, as he saw them all climbing the few steps to the hotel reception.

Before they got to top of the stairs Christos had Anton in a bear hug and was motioning to his wife to come over.

Anna, who had been carrying a large tray full of silk flowers, came over and welcomed Anton in a more dignified way of kissing him on both cheeks.

'Anton, my dear friend. It's so good to see you again. You are looking a bit thin, maybe you are not eating enough. Go over to see Eleni and she will feed you. Don't you think he needs feeding up, Christos?'

'Oh leave him alone Anna' laughed Christos. 'I'm sure he's eating plenty, He's been on a cruise for the last 2 weeks for goodness sake! So, Anton, are you not going to introduce us to your friends then?'

'Of course I am' laughed Anton. 'And yes, it's wonderful to see you both too. Anyway, this is Sally and her husband Mike who I met on the cruise that we've been on. This is our last port of call before we disembark in Corfu tomorrow and fly home!'

Both Christos and Anna hugged and kissed Sally and Mike and then motioned for them all to come over to the restaurant.

'Come, let's have some coffee and cake' said Anna leading the way to the outdoor restaurant. 'As you can see we are pretty busy organising for a wedding that is being held here later this afternoon. In fact you may know the happy couple, Andrea and Jack. They normally come out around this time or sometimes in June with another couple, Sid and Elaine. I'm sure they've been out here when you've been here'

'Yes, I do remember them' said Anton pulling out a chair for Sally to sit in the shade of the restaurant, which although was outside, was shaded by enormous umbrellas and overhead vines. 'You'd get on well with them Sally, they live out your way, Brentwood I think and Sid and Elaine live in Chelmsford if I remember rightly. Andrea's daughter owns an Italian restaurant not far from where they live. Sophie, isn't it?'

'Yes, that's right' agreed Anna. 'I think Andrea's first husband and Sophie's father was an Italian chef. That's where she gets her love of food from.'

'It's such a shame we couldn't stay here later and have a peek at them getting married but we have to be back on board ship by 4.30.

You'll have to get Petros to put some pictures of it all on Facebook. Talking of which, where is he?'

'Actually, I think he is with Jack and Andrea now, sorting out the table plans and stuff. I'm sure he will be popping over here shortly to pick up the flowers that Anna has been arranging for the tables. Right, who's for coffee and cake and maybe some Ouzo?'

Christos went into the restaurant and came out laden down with homemade honey cake, a jug of freshly brewed coffee and a bottle of Ouzo, complete with half a dozen shot glasses. He also had his daughter Eleni with him, who he had dragged away from the kitchen where she was prepping for the wedding and this evenings' service. She looked quite annoyed that her father had insisted she come outside but when she saw Anton her face lit up.

'Hey, Anton, what the hell are you doing here? I thought that you were on some amazing cruise?'

'I am Eleni, but seeing as the ship has docked in Zakynthos, where better to spend my day than with you wonderful people. So how is the best chef in Greece?'

Eleni blushed but Anton could see she was bursting with pride.

'I don't know she's got the day off. But she left me, just a humble Greek cook, in charge of the kitchen, can you believe it!'

'You, a humble Greek cook. In your dreams! This from a lady who learnt her trade in New York under one of the greatest chefs in the US! These are my friends Sally and Mike, by the way. We met on the cruise and have been inseparable since!

Sally, Mike. This is Eleni, Christos and Anna's daughter and chef of this wonderful restaurant.'

Once all the introductions were out of the way, Anna cut up the cake and handed it round and Christos served everyone a coffee and an Ouzo.

'Yammas. To our good friend Anton and to our new friends Sally and Mike'

'Yammas' said everyone, drinking the shots of Ouzo down in one.

'Ah, here comes Petros and Anita' laughter Christos. 'Word has obviously got around that you are here, no!'

'No, more likely they've smelled Anna's famous honey cake' laughed Anton.

Once again, there were introductions, hugs, kisses and yet more Ouzo to toast everyone!

'Did Dad tell you that we are preparing for Andrea and Jack's wedding this afternoon?' said Petros, pouring himself some coffee.

'Yes he did, it's about time he made an honest woman of her. They must have been coming out here some years now. I remember them from back when I was coming out here with Kenny'

'Yeah, you're right, it has been a few years now. Actually I've just left them over at the wedding pavilion going over the table plans. I think they wanted some time away from the rest of the party. They've got all the relatives out for the wedding and it's obvious that some of them really don't get on well. I reckon by the time the wedding is over, they'll need a holiday to get over it!'

'I think they're staying on for a few more days after everyone else has gone home for that reason!' said Anita, stuffing sugared almonds into netting to make the favours.

'They'll definitely need it I think' agreed Petros. 'Right we'd better be getting back over there as we've still got loads to do. Why don't you pop over there with us Anton and say hello. I'm sure they'd be really upset if they knew you were here and hadn't seen them.'

'That's a good idea, I think I will. Why don't you two come over there as well?' Anton asked Sally and Mike. 'The wedding pavilion is really pretty and you can meet Andrea and Jack. Then perhaps we can have a walk round the resort before having some lunch back here in the restaurant. Unless you wanted to do something different?'

'No, that sounds absolutely perfect' said Sally. 'As long as you're sure you want us following you around everywhere!'

'Of course I do sweetie. It's great showing you off to all my friends here. I just hope you are enjoying yourself!'

'We're having a great day so far Anton. This is a gorgeous hotel and your friends are wonderful. I've got a feeling we may be coming back here one day for a holiday!'

They finished their coffees and made their way over to the pavilion which was located at the back of the hotel in the beautiful manicured gardens. Anton was right when he said it was pretty. The actual area where the wedding was taking place was a large, white and blue wooden pergola with white washed decking. This was draped with white organza which was set off by masses of purple bougainvillea which was trained around the roof of the pergola. Dotted inside were arrangements of mauve, purple and white freesias, lilies and roses, which matched perfectly with the colour scheme that the bridal party had chosen.

The tables for the wedding breakfast spanned out from the main pergola and were also amass with the same flowers. The tables were in the middle of being set up and were looking beautiful with pristine white tablecloths and white china on gold chargers. Sparkling glasswear and stunning table arrangements completed the striking but classic look that everyone had been striving to achieve.

Anton spotted Andrea and Jack standing inside the main pergola chatting to Anita, who was putting the finishing touches to the seating plan. Jack was the first to see him and waved him over.

'Hey Anton, me old mate. How are you? Long-time no see. Are you staying here?'

'Hiya Jack, Andrea. I'm fine thanks. No I'm not staying here, I'm actually on a cruise with these 2 lovely people who I met on board. Sally, Mike, this is Jack and Andrea, the couple who are getting married.'

They all greeted each other and sat down at one of the tables.

I can't believe you've finally managed to get him down the aisle, Andrea!' laughed Anton

'No, neither can I. It's about time that's for sure. So you're on a cruise are you? How the other half live. Whereabouts are you going?'

'More like where we've been actually, as this is our last port of call. It was a cruise all around the Greek islands and it has been absolutely fabulous.'

'Didn't you say before you were going on a cruise like that with Kenny?' asked Jack.

'Yes you're right, we were supposed to go on this same ship for our 30th anniversary weren't we, then when he got ill he made me promise to go without him. So that's what I did. Anyway, how's the wedding planning going? Petros said you were getting a bit stressed over it.'

'It's not the wedding we're getting stressed over' said Jack, 'it's the guests. Remind me never to have all my family and friends in one place ever again, it's a total recipe for disaster. I actually wish that we'd come away on our own and done it now but I'm sure it will be alright on the night, so to speak!'

'I'm sure it will. Just last minute nerves for everyone I suppose. It's a shame we have to be back on the ship by 4.30 as I'd have loved to have seen you all in your finery. Still, Petros said he will take loads of pictures to put on Facebook.'

'Yeah, it is a shame you won't be here later. Sid and Elaine will be gutted that they've missed you. They've gone into town to pick up the last bits and bobs. The ceremony is at 4.30 so you wouldn't be able to even catch a bit of it. We chose a later time so it wouldn't be quite so hot.'

'I don't blame you, I certainly wouldn't want to be suited and booted in this heat. Well it's been lovely seeing you both, I really hope your big day goes well and I'll look forward to seeing all the pictures. I'm sure you've got loads to be getting on with so we'll leave you in peace now and I'm sure we can catch up some other time.'

They all said their goodbyes and wished the happy couple good luck and then made their way back over to the reception where they told Christos that they were going for a little wander round the resort and would be back for lunch at around 12.30.

After walking around the shops and buying a few last minute trinkets to remind them of Zakynthos they all walked down to the beach to dip their toes into the warm, clear waters of the Ionian Sea and take a few pictures of their last port of call.

'It's very quiet down here' notice Sally. 'There's no bars or music playing. There's not even any water sports. I always thought this was a right lively resort.'

'No, you're thinking of Laganas just along the bay there. That's full of bars and clubs. This beach is actually part of the National Marine Park as it's the nesting place of the Loggerhead turtles, or Caretta Caretta as they call them here. Because the turtles are now endangered, all music, bars and water sports are banned. In fact the beach is closed off at night completely. It actually makes a nice change to lay on a beach and just listen to the sound of the waves lapping rather than banging music or speedboats revving up. You should come here earlier in the year and chances are you will be swimming and a turtle will pop up beside you as the bay is full of them.

'Oh wow' exclaimed Sally. 'That's amazing. I love turtles. That's it, another place we'll have to come back to!'

Before walking back to the hotel they bought some frappes from Spiros, the guy who ran the refreshments van at the entrance to the beach and sat chatting to him for a while. Anton explained how he knew him, as this was where he always bought his lunch when he was on the beach. Spiros then told them all that he also now had a couple of villas, that were halfway between the beach and the hotel, that he rented out and gave them all some cards in case they wanted to stay there some time. Sally made a fuss of his two dogs who were jumping all over her, desperate for her to play with them and Mike bought a couple of sausages to give them as treats. The Greeks, as usual, looked at them as if they were totally mad!

Once they had finished their frappes and said their goodbyes, they took a slow walk back in readiness for some lunch.

By the time they reached the hotel, they had built up quite an appetite and were really looking forward to having something to eat. The food in the hotel's restaurant certainly didn't disappoint. The menu wasn't enormous, with a selection of around 10 different starters, 20 mains and whatever desserts were on the board that day, but the menu changed frequently, depending on what was in season. Eleni liked to keep the food as fresh as she could so tried, wherever possible, to use food that was seasonal and not to rely on anything frozen.

As all three of them loved fish, they decided to push the boat out and have the fish platter, which included whitebait, prawns, calamari and selection of fish. It came on a massive plate for them to share, complete with a bowl of seasoned chips, a large Greek salad and some freshly baked bread. The fish was cooked to perfection and there wasn't a thing left at the end, apart from a few bones and a bit of bread.

After they had finished eating, they were joined by Christos and Anna who treated them to coffee and Ouzos before, all too soon it was time for them to call a taxi and get back to the ship. They said their goodbyes to the family, who sent them on their way with some of Eleni's homemade Baklava, a couple of bottles of Christos' homemade wine and a bottle of Ouzo. All three of them promised faithfully that they would return one day.

Chapter 24

They got back to the ship with only a few minutes to spare and stood on the sun deck watching as the Grecian Princess slipped out to sea one last time, sadly waving goodbye to Zakynthos.

As it was their last night on board ship, they were all going to be eating together in the main dining room and had previously arranged to meet up in the usual bar at around 7.30.

Mike and Sally got back to their cabin at around 5.15, had quick showers then finished packing ready to disembark the next morning. The cases were to be left outside the cabins that evening, where they would be collected and taken to the airport ready for their flight home. They left out just the bare essentials for the following morning. This, and their clothes from that evening, could then be packed in their small carry on cases.

'I can't believe this is our last night' said Sally looking wistfully out at the sparkling, blue Ionian Sea. 'It seems like only yesterday we were getting on, all excited about what cruising would be like and worried whether we would take to it or not and now we're packing to go home. I think we need to book another holiday when we get back to take the sting out of it!'

'Sounds like a good idea babe. We'll get some brochures on our drive back. I don't know about you but I've had a fabulous holiday and I'd definitely do this cruising malarkey again, wouldn't you?'

'Definitely. This has got to be one of the best holiday I've had' agreed Sally. 'The ship is just pure luxury, the food is outstanding and we've been to some amazing places and met some wonderful people. I will be really sad to say goodbye to all this.'

'I know, but we have made some great friends and I'm sure we'll stay in contact with them. Talking of which, we'd better get a move on if we're meeting everyone at 7.30!'

They put the last bits in the cases and put them outside the door then came back in and got changed, making it to the bar just behind Simon and Candice, who had already ordered a round of drinks.

The last night was a bitter sweet occasion, as everyone agreed they had all had a fabulous holiday and were really sad to be going home and leaving the good friends that they had made. There was a frenzied exchange of addresses, phone numbers and e-mails at the bar, along with promises that they would all stay in touch. After a couple more cocktails they headed, for the last time, into The Parthenon for dinner.

'I'm really going to miss this' said Richard as their waiter put a plate of lobster thermidor in front of him. 'Back to egg and chips in front of the telly next week, I suppose!'

'I know, I think we are all going to come back down to earth with a bump after this!' said Simon, tucking into his quail!

Once they had all finished eating, they moved into The Medusa Bar for coffees and liqueurs, sitting chatting amicably for an hour or so before, saying their goodnights and making their way back to their cabins for a relatively early night.

They had agreed to meet up for breakfast the last day at around 7.30, as Anton, Valerie, Richard and Hannah had a 9.00 disembarkation time. The rest of them were disembarking right behind at 9.30 and catching their coaches to the airport. Valerie was going straight to a hotel in Corfu Town, where she would be meeting up with Fergus and spending a week, getting to know him better in the sun. She had finally come clean about him the previous evening and everyone was really happy for her and Fergus, who they thought made a wonderful couple.

Anton, Simon and Candice were flying back to Gatwick at 1.30 and Sally, Mike, Richard and Hannah were right behind them at 2 o'clock, flying into Stansted.

When Sally and Mike got to the dining room the next morning the rest of them were already there. They were shown to their table and ordered the full works, as they knew not to expect anything in the way of decent food at the airport. Sally sneaked a couple of Danish pastries into her handbag for the journey and Hannah and Candice followed suit after watching her.

They hoped to see each other at some point at the airport but just in case they didn't, they all said their goodbyes after breakfast. There were lots of hugs, kisses and tears and promises of phone calls as soon as they all got home.

Sally and Mike, along with Simon and Candice made their way to the disembarkation area that they had been given and sat and waited for the call to exit. They didn't have to wait too long before the doors were opened and they made their way through to where everyone was now leaving. Coaches were lined up at the bottom of the gangway and they finally found the right coach number and got on board.

There was a wait of around 20 minutes while everyone got on and then they made the journey back to Corfu Airport where their plane home awaited.

After a non-eventful flight back to the UK, they managed to say their goodbyes once more to Hannah and Richard, who they caught up with at Passport Control. Once all their cases had been safely retrieved, they made their way to the long term car park, where they picked up their car and drove the 45 minute journey back home to Essex.

Once home, the first thing they did, after unpacking and putting a load of washing on, was to get on-line and start looking at the next holiday they could book!

~ **The End** ~

Epilogue

True to their word, Sally and Mike booked another holiday as soon as they got home. In fact they booked several over the course of the next year or so – a fortnight in Cyprus to see Lucy, a week back in Kefalonia and another 2 cruises, one to the Norwegian Fjords and one to the Caribbean. They stayed in contact with everyone they met on the cruise and have already spent a couple of weekends with Simon and Candice and Anton, as well as meeting up with everyone at the christening.

After Mike met up with Rick, they both keep in contact via the cruise forums, of which Mike is now a member of the Admin team!

Hannah and Richard gave birth to healthy twin girls, who they named Sally-Ann and Abigail. The whole crowd turned up for the christening, which turned into a great reunion weekend for everyone. They all adored the babies and couldn't believe the change in Hannah, who seemed to have taken to motherhood like a duck to water. Sally and Mike see them quite regularly at their home in Suffolk, as they can pop in on the way through when Mike visits his Dad.

Anton is still doing his charity work and has started to see one of the volunteers he works with, a semi-retired author in his 50's called Gareth. It's early days yet, but he has already introduced him to Sally and Mike and they love him.

Simon and Candice got their dog Lara from Crete and absolutely adore her. They are now looking to adopt another dog from the same shelter and are going back out there soon. Simon is on track to get his number one salesman award again this year and Candice is looking to expand her business premises but also to employ some more staff so she can relax a bit more.

Valerie and Fergus spent a week in Corfu after the cruise and got on like a house on fire. Fergus did one more cruise then took early retirement and has moved to Norfolk where he is working with Valerie at Nom Noms, the café she owns in Norwich.

Prudence and George were last seen getting into a taxi at Gatwick Airport with Roy and his wife!

Jack and Andreas wedding in Zakynthos went without a hitch and they lived happily ever after – or did they?

If you want to find out exactly what happened, you'll have to wait for my next book, which is set in Zakynthos and follows the stories of all the guests at Jack and Andrea's wedding at the Ionian Dream.

About the Author

Debbie is originally from Essex but moved to Norfolk around 16 years ago. She works as a legal secretary at a firm of local solicitors and lives with her husband of 23 years and their two Cocker Spaniels.

It was being made redundant from her previous job that enabled her to treat both her and her husband to their first cruise. This gave her the inspiration to write "It's all Greek at Sea" and now there is no stopping her! Debbie has already started her second book, which is set on her favourite Greek island, Zakynthos and there are another 3 books in the pipeline which will all feature at least one character from her first book.

Apart from writing, Debbie is an avid reader and enjoys books from varying genres, including thrillers, horror and holiday based fiction. She also enjoys cooking for family and friends, travelling abroad on holiday, trying to learn Greek and listening to music.

If you would like to find out more about Debbie then check out her Facebook page on www.facebook.com/debbieward-author.

Printed in Great Britain
by Amazon